Rice AND Beans

Valerie Taylor

The Naiad Press, Inc.
1989

Printed in the United States of America
First Edition

Edited by Christine Cassidy
Cover design by Pat Tong and Bonnie Liss
    (Phoenix Graphics)
Typeset by Sandi Stancil

Library of Congress Cataloging-in-Publication Data

Taylor, Valerie, 1913—
    Rice and beans / by Valerie Taylor.
        p.   cm.
    ISBN 0-941483-41-X : $8.95
    I. Title.
PS3570.A957R5   1989
813'.54--dc20   89-33964
                                                           CIP

This book is dedicated to my son, James Tate, the only person I know who is brave enough to read my first-draft typing.

About the Author

Valerie Taylor was born Velma Nacella Young in Aurora, Illinois, in 1913 — a period when dinosaurs still roamed the earth. She grew up in a mostly rural and populist atmosphere and after a normal period of rebellion against the family, settled into supporting gay rights, socialism, world peace, refugee sanctuary and good cooking. She attended Blackburn College at Carlinville, Illinois for two years and taught country school for a while before making a disastrous marriage. After ending the marriage in 1953 she supported her three sons by office work, editing and ad-writing, and also by writing confession stories at night.

She has published about 300 poems and a variety of short pieces. *Rice and Beans* is her thirteenth published book, not counting reprints and translations. At present she is stuck halfway through a new story and has two more in the back of her mind.

Chapter 1

The fluorescent lights in the Department of Economic Security office looked pale and watery after the outdoor glare. Marty stood blinking in the doorway, taking it in. Grimly pale green walls, shiny molded plastic chairs bolted together in threes, a rack of pamphlets — EAT RIGHT TO BE HEALTHY. At one side a waist-high partition topped with wire netting, behind which three women stood doing nothing: a busty chemical blonde, a nervous-looking thin lady in ruffles, and a sleepy Chicana. Institutional was the word. Mental hospitals, clinics,

1

employment agencies all looked like this. They even had a dry, papery smell all their own.

She sat down in the nearest chair. Three other applicants were waiting, one a woman of sixty who looked like her third-grade teacher and had dolled up for the interview, wore a hat and a trim skirt and blouse. Didn't she know they would turn her down if she looked middle-class? Behind her sat a thin black girl far gone in pregnancy. A baby every year, Marty's mind jeered, so as to get all those big fat welfare checks. At the back of the room a thin young woman had her face in a book. Readers were scarce in Marty's considerable experience with do-gooding. She tried to read the title, but it was hidden and she didn't want to look like she was staring. She swiveled around and fixed her gaze on the blank front wall.

The young black woman slid out of her chair and sauntered over to the wire cage in cheap pointy purple flats. Her stance said, I've waited long enough; you bitches are supposed to be here for my benefit. Marty felt a grin on her face and wiped it off in a hurry.

From a wall speaker a dry impersonal male voice said, "You are entitled to be treated with respect. But respect goes with honesty. Please fill out all of the spaces in your case book. Answer them truthfully. You are entitled to be treated with respect." Something was missing. After a puzzled moment she identified it: no Spanish follow-up. Seventy miles from the border, in a town where you couldn't get a job in a hospital or department store unless you were bilingual, the government was conducting its business entirely in English; and its business was feeding the hungry, who had a tendency to belong to minority

2

groups. If they didn't understand, that was their hard luck.

The girl in the purple shoes said, "I want to see about getting me some food stamps."

The Chicana handed her a fat booklet from a wire basket of them, careful not to look at her or touch her hand. "Fill it in and bring it back. Don't skip anything." It was at least thirty pages, Marty guessed, as she stood up and went to stand beside the wood-and-wire cage. What in hell do they want to know, your family history back to Adam?

She was wordlessly handed one of the booklets. "You got a pen?" Nobody answered. She turned back, took two more booklets and handed them out to the ex-schoolteacher and the girl with the book. The blonde gave her a sour look. This wasn't the way they did it, this wasn't according to regs. You are entitled to be treated with contempt.

The young woman with the book said, "Here, I think I have —" and opened her little plastic purse. Everything fell out — comb, lipstick, change purse, rumpled tissue and, rolling over the floor, a cheap ballpoint. Marty stooped and picked the stuff up. The girl said in a thin shaky voice, "Thanks," and handed her the pen. Marty looked at the case workers. Maybe it was against the rules to talk.

The blonde said, bored, "Anybody need any help with their questionnaire?" Nobody did. Nobody would who wasn't totally illiterate. Name, address, zip code, telephone. Somebody had told her that you couldn't qualify unless you had a fixed address and a phone; that was meant to weed out transients who were flocking to the Sun Belt by the thousands to keep from freezing to death.

3

She skipped the first page and rifled through the rest of it; then, not believing her own eyes, went back to the beginning and looked again. Nice little book, thirty-six pages, glossy paper, English only. And what questions!

How many people live in your house? List their names, ages, relationships, places of employment, welfare benefits they receive, weekly wages. How many own cars? Have bank accounts, are on Social Security, are on strike?

How much cash do you have on hand? Do you own a car, real estate, jewelry or other assets, other property? Does anyone eat with you? Does anyone give you food? Money? List savings accounts, pensions, other sources of income. Do you expect to receive money in the near future, from insurance, an inheritance, payment of a debt?'

Just a few things they missed, Marty thought, trying to distract herself from the printed columns because she could feel anger boiling up in her. Do you have any birthmarks? Do you wear pajamas or a nightgown? How many times a day do you pee?

The black girl was filling in spaces, looking cool. She had done this before, had her answers ready, probably had her rent receipts, phone bills, tax returns and medical records all laid out at home, ready to attach. Utility bills — how many people had receipted utility bills? How many people had rent receipts, if it came to that? You paid by the week, and if you missed a week the landlord threw you out. As for tax returns, Marty had never filed one in her life. All the picky little jobs she had held didn't add up to that much. Anyway, if you babysat or did housework you were paid under the table; nobody ever reported it.

She capped the ballpoint and stuck it in her pocket. "Can I take this home and finish it?" The three women behind the wire looked at her like teachers sizing up a sassy pupil. The Chicana asked, "Do you want some help?"

"No, I'm just gong to check out some of the answers." Fake out some of the answers was what she meant, but she tried to look polite. She was on her feet and aimed at the door.

The wall speaker was still going on about dignity and honesty. She supposed if you worked there, you got so you didn't hear it.

She stepped out into the sunshine, which hit her in the face like a blowtorch. I need sunglasses, she reminded herself for the hundredth time. But sunglasses were at least five dollars a pair, even the ones you bought off a rack in the supermarket. Anyway, it was good to be out of that place, like getting out of the hospital and feeling free and loose in the good old germy air.

"Hey, wait a minute!"

She paused, teetering a little because the space between the DES building and the sidewalk was covered with large rounded stones. Great for people with crutches and wheelchairs, Marty thought. The thin girl who had lent her the pen was teetering across them, a little unsteadily, clutching her form book and little purse. "Oh! I have your pen."

"That's all right," the girl said apologetically, as if she were the one at fault.

She looked even smaller and thinner in the

sunlight, with one leg a little shorter than the other; she teetered a little as she walked. Par for the course. Old people, handicapped, pregnant girls in slippery soles, nobody gave a damn. But this one looked cheerful enough now that she had caught up with Marty. "I'm sorry, I don't understand the questions. Do you? I don't know all those things."

"Nobody does," Marty assured her. "Come on, let's cross on the light. This town is full of crazy drivers. Let's get out of the sun before we both drop dead." She slowed down a little to let her new friend catch up. "Let's go and sit on the bus bench. There's a ramada over it, a little roof."

They waited for the light, crossed, and sat down on the bench, away from the sights and sounds of bureaucracy at work. They looked at each other. Marty saw a small, too-thin young woman in her early twenties, with clear blue eyes and stringy fair hair soaked with sweat. Her slacks and tee shirt could have come from any discount store or resale shop; they were faded and tacky. She was shaking a little from tension or fatigue or the hundred-degree heat, no way to tell.

Marty didn't need a mirror to know how people saw her. Sturdily built and a little taller than average, with a chopped-off haircut and nothing-much eyes, a good Arizona tan, chambray shirt with sleeves reefed, old jeans, secondhand jogging shoes. Butch. Or tomboy, depending on how much you knew about her kind of woman.

The scrutiny was getting embarrassing. She said, "My name's Marty. Really Martha, but I like Marty better."

"I'm Althea. I was named for my grandmother."

"That's a pretty name."

"My friends call me Thea. Did. I don't have any friends here. I was at the U for a while, but my grant ran out before I got acquainted. University's too big anyhow, you never get to know anyone."

"You from away?" Because almost everybody was. The first two questions were, "Hot enough for you?" and "Where you from?"

"Jersey. I always wanted to live someplace where it didn't snow in winter, but there's no jobs here."

"Backward state," Marty said briefly. "No industry. No unions to speak of. They got a right-to-starve law. Fiftieth in health care, down near the bottom in school systems, and everybody's here because if you have to be poor, it's better to be poor in a warm climate."

"Yeah. I saw a piece about it in the paper. Men sleeping in junky old cars — old ladies with their stuff in shopping bags — shanties made out of cardboard boxes. I guess they don't freeze, though."

"Sometimes they die of heatstroke."

A bus stopped. Marty shook her head; the driver pulled away. "Where do you live?"

"North and east — for now. My rent's up tomorrow."

"You should have started with general assistance. How long you been here?"

"About eight months."

"No good. Takes a year to establish residency. They won't give you anything, not general assistance or food stamps or their fake Medicaid — this is the only state in the Union that doesn't have Medicaid. You can throw that little book away."

Thea said in a small voice, "How do people live?"

"Some don't," Marty said harshly. "Some get food from the churches or the Sallies. Some go on the streets. There's an awful lot of whores in this town, some of them are so homely you'd wonder, but they never seem to run out of customers. Most of them would sooner be working in a convenience store or on an assembly line — not that there's many assembly lines, this is a tourist town. The copper mines have closed down and the Air Force base only hires a few people. Some men go on the harvest crews, but that's a Mexican job, a wetback job because of the inflation there. Ranchers don't have to pay legal minimum."

"What do you do, yourself?"

"My last job was a Circle K. Graveyard shift. Two guys came in one night and shot the other clerk and the manager. I was in the john. The other clerk was a guy I was riding with — the buses stop at eight o'clock. Not that I was too crazy about working there, anymore." She smiled, without humor. "Still makes me throw up when I think about it."

Thea's eyes filled with tears, whether for Marty, the murdered man, or herself, Marty didn't know. She said as cheerfully as she could, "Never mind, something will happen. It always does."

"Sure," Althea said with unexpected bitterness. "I'm going back where I'm staying and pack my suitcase. Only I never saw a bag lady with a suitcase, they mostly carry plastic shopping bags. There's a couple that hang around the downtown bus stop —"

"Sniping butts. When you don't have anything to eat, a cigarette kind of eases the hunger. And that reminds me, I got a dollar stashed away, folding money I mean, besides my bus fare. Now what I'd really like is a hamburger with everything, but we

8

could get an order of fries and split it. If you're not worried about calories."

"I haven't had many lately," Thea said with a glimmer of a smile. "Probably wouldn't recognize one if I saw it."

She followed Marty to McDonalds, but waited outside. The fries smelled wonderful. Still — "I don't think I should eat them. You can't afford to feed me."

"So what?" They reclaimed their bench. Marty spread out two paper napkins and divided the fries scrupulously, giving Thea the biggest ones. "Eat it in good health."

"Finger-licking good," Althea said, trying not to gobble, trying to eat slowly and make it last.

When they had licked the last grain of salt from their fingers Thea came back to the questionnaire, which she was still clutching. "How do you fill these out?"

"Well, it's a Catch-22. If you tell the truth they say you don't qualify. If you lie and they catch you, you still don't qualify. The idea is to keep from spending the state's money. They're cutting down on everything except politicians' salaries."

"Some people get food stamps. I see them all the time, in stores."

"People with ten kids. People who know their alderman. Or really good liars, I suppose. Some people get disability pensions or SSI, too. I'm no good at that stuff."

Another bus came along. Thea stood up uncertainly. Marty said, "Look, I got a place to stay. It's not much of a place, but you're welcome to stay there if you want. The lady can't afford to feed me

— she has four kids and no husband — but she wouldn't throw you out. She's some kind of a shirttail relation to my mother."

"You don't even know me."

"You don't know me, either." Marty climbed onto the bus and waited, fare in hand, while Thea got on. "Where do you live? I hope it's in walking distance of my stop, because this is my last money. I couldn't go back to DES if I wanted to."

Thea's rooming house turned out to be about an eight-block walk. "See, we're lucky," Marty said. "I wish my feet wouldn't get so tired, that's all I wish."

Chapter 2

Marty didn't get much sleep that night. The half-order of fries, salty and oily, stirred up her appetite, and her stomach cramped with emptiness. It wouldn't have been so bad if she could have looked forward to breakfast, but as far as she could see there was no food at all in her future. The supermarket down the street, its shelves lined with thousands of things to eat, filled her thoughts. If I had a dollar I'd buy something, maybe a loaf of bread, and steal a chunk of cheese or some cold cuts, she thought; but you couldn't walk into a store and leave without buying something, they were on the lookout for thieves.

The single bed was too narrow for two, even though Thea slept politely on the outside edge with one arm dangling over the side. And it was a hot night. Marty had gone to bed in her underpants and tee shirt, as a courtesy. Now she longed to strip off the sweaty garments and feel what breeze there was. She shut her eyes and tried to sleep, but it was no use.

It was no time to think about anything but basics — tonight, how to get cooled off; tomorrow, where to find something to eat. Threaded through these worries was the consciousness of another woman lying beside her. She didn't know Thea, had just met her for the first time, and she had never gone for those thin pale girls anyway, but it was a long time since she had been close to anyone, and that special feeling was beginning to bother her. Come to think of it, Thea looked a little like Eileen, who had brought her out when she was in the psych ward. Younger than Eileen and without her humorous, sure-of-herself look, but with the same cast of features. Thinking about Eileen and their brief unsatisfying encounters on the grounds and in the linen room deepened and localized the feeling that was nagging at her, the feeling of wanting someone. She considered getting out of bed, tiptoeing into the bathroom and dealing with it there, but she would probably wake Thea and she would almost certainly wake Aunt Susan who was a light sleeper, or one of the kids would have to go. She lay still, with an achy tiredness in her arms and shoulders and itchy sweat trickling down her back, hungry for sleep but unable to turn off her thoughts.

What would Thea say if she put a hand on her? Alone with a dyke, in bed with a dyke — wow! Most straight women knew about the sexual revolution, they were all for it in principle, they read *Cosmo*, but when it came to having somebody make a pass at them — especially if that somebody was a woman — well, it was like marrying a Negro, nice to be broad-minded where someone else's kids were concerned, but not for yours. She could imagine Thea climbing out of bed, skinning into her clothes and getting out of there. Out into the hot night, where muggers and rapists lurked, and no place to go. There was a shelter for homeless men now, an old falling-down building taken over by a few determined young people over the protests of their neighbors, but it was always overflowing and there was no place, even there, for a girl. A young girl. The bag ladies all seemed to be seventy or older, and they slept with one eye open if they slept at all.

This was the only safe place for Thea. Marty knew she couldn't do or say anything to scare her away.

Panhandling was easier for men, too. You couldn't get off a bus downtown without some skinny kid with a backpack asking for a little change. Some stood on the street corners playing guitar, or just holding out a cap in the hope that someone would drop a dime or quarter into it. She had been approached in the shopping plaza by a girl, asking for money to buy diapers — but the baby she carried looked well-fed and clean, and nobody was giving. Marty had sized her up as lazy or smart-aleck.

There was whoring. She might have tried to turn a trick, pushing down her nausea at the thought of contact with a man and her fear of AIDS and herpes, but Oracle Road was lined with pretty kids who looked like high school students, earning their twenty bucks a time. She'd never stand up against that kind of competition.

God, I wish I had a hamburger, Marty thought. A nice thick juicy hamburger on a sesame bun, with mustard and ketchup and pickle and a slice of onion. There was a time when she used to leave the top half of the bun on the plate, in the hope of getting thin. She wished she had one of those wasted buns.

She must have fallen asleep, because suddenly the sun was shining in and she opened her eyes to see Thea sitting on the edge of the bed, dressed and looking scared. "What time is it?"

"Around seven, I think. Is it all right if I use the bathroom?"

Marty laughed. "If you can get in. There's Aunt Susan and the four kids and a guy who boards here — I think they live on his board money, mostly. If you want a bath you'll have to wait till later." To make conversation, and because she felt some kind of explanation was called for, she added, "She isn't really my aunt — I guess I told you that. Nor is the boarder her boyfriend or anything like that. She's very religious. Strictly business." Marty sat up and stretched. The morning breeze was still coming in at the window; it felt good. "There, someone just came out. You can get in before the next one."

She dressed quickly while Thea was out of the room, and took her turn at the john to give her a few moments of privacy.

Washed and with her fair hair pulled back in a ponytail and tied with a ribbon, Thea looked even

14

younger than in the DES office. And not bad looking though her right arm and right leg were a little smaller than the left and she walked with a sort of controlled limp. She would have looked like a teenager with a little meat on her bones.

"How old are you, anyhow?"

"Twenty-three. I'm an Aries."

"I'm a Taurus, and that's a lot of bull. I don't believe that stuff. I'm thirty-one." It was like an introduction. Marty felt that they knew each other now.

"What are we going to do today? I can't go back to that place. What does DES stand for, anyhow?"

"Department of Economic Security. Ain't that a trip?"

"I can't go back there even if I starve to death."

"Wouldn't do you any good if you did. You have to be an educated liar. You gotta remember though, those people aren't bad. It's just a job, low pay but good fringe benefits and a pension to look forward to. If they didn't have that job they might be in the same fix we're in. They're like nurses, they can't get personal about it."

"In a way, that makes it worse."

"Or they're like guys drafted into the army. If you thought about the guys on the other side as human beings you couldn't stand it."

A racket started up outside. Marty pulled up the shade. "That bunch next door is going someplace. Probably been up all night." Two boys and three girls in shorts stood around an old car which was puffing clouds of smoke and making odd noises. The one who seemed to be in charge had a green Mohawk and a torn tee shirt that left his bellybutton bare. "They

drive Aunt Susan crazy. Party all night, smoke pot —
she says — and walk around with ghetto-blasters.
There's new ones coming and going all the time."

"A commune?"

"I don't think they're that organized. It's just a
pad where kids flop. Runaways, probably. There's a
lot of that around."

She yelled out of the window, "What's the
problem?"

The green-haired boy looked up. "She won't
start."

"Wait a minute, let me take a look at her."

"I think she just died on us, but you're welcome
to try."

Thea followed her down the back stairs, past the
breakfast noises from behind the kitchen door. "If I
was your aunt I'd ask you to breakfast," she said
crossly, and Marty laughed.

"Take the food out of her kids' mouths? She
figures I can look after myself, big healthy chick like
me."

The five in the yard looked at them without
speaking. Marty got into the car, and turned off the
ignition. "You've flooded her. Where did you get this
heap, anyhow?"

The green-haired boy looked at her, and away.
"We sort of came into possession of her."

"I bet. Wait a minute and I'll try again."

It was a clear morning, a good day to stand
around in someone's yard and visit. One of the girls
asked, "Where you two going so early in the
morning?"

"Thought we might walk down behind the
supermarket and see what they've thrown out. I

16

found half a crate of lettuce one time. Just wilted a little bit."

There was an interchange of looks among the five. The girl said, "No food, I guess. No money either."

"We applied for food stamps. Nice try, but no cigar."

Apparently the five had reached a consensus without saying anything. "We're going for food boxes. You wanna come along? It's a church, but no bullshit. You sign your name and they give you this stuff."

"Can you get us in this heap? That's if she starts."

"Always room for more."

The car started, strangling a little. She groaned and clanked, and Marty wondered why the springs didn't break with seven people stuffed in, but they moved out into the street and roared away. Marty sat in back with Thea on her lap, the youngest girl squeezed up against her. She could have driven the heap better than the Mohawk boy, but knew better than to say so. It was only a dozen blocks or so; they pulled up in front of a big brick church and filed into a side door, down a flight of stairs and into a big room with rows of folding chairs and a small organ. Sunday school, church suppers. At the far end, in front of a sliding window which undoubtedly led to a kitchen, cardboard cartons and stacks of cans and boxes were piled on a long folding table. Two pleasant-looking middle-aged women sat alongside.

"You're new, aren't you? Do you live together?"

"We live in the same building, but we're not related." That was the truth, but Marty felt as if she were deceiving these women. She filled out her index

17

card: name, address and phone number, easier than thinking up thirty-six pages of believable answers to intrusive questions.

The women began dealing foods into five cardboard cartons, and the boys started out with them. The taller lady, who might have been the minister's wife or the head of the Ladies Aid, asked, "Does anyone else live with either of you? Where there are children, we like to put in something a little extra."

"No, no children."

"We'd be pleased to have you come to Sunday morning service. Only if you want to, of course." She shoved a box towards Marty. "Come back in two weeks if you're still out of work. Now you're on the list, we'll have something ready for you."

Thea said, "Thank you very much," like a good little girl accepting a birthday present.

The boy with the Mohawk came back in to carry Thea's box. "If they'd put it in two, I'd carry one," she said unhappily.

He gave her a cold look. "No sweat. Get in the car."

There was no way seven people and five big cartons could ride in that worn-out jalopy. The boy with the Mohawk, emerging finally as the leader, motioned at Thea. "You, get in. You" — to Marty — "and you guys can walk."

That was nice of him, Marty thought. Anyone could see that Thea was handicapped, but not everyone would have let her ride. Marty said, "Go ahead, I'll be there before long." She and the other girls and the skinniest of the boys started out on foot. Not one of them was a day over twenty. Marty

18

said, "That was nice of you to tell us about the place. If we can do anything for you, yell."

"She your chick?"

"Just a friend." Since yesterday, she thought, but had sense enough not to say.

One of the girls said, "Timmy's kind-hearted." Her voice was possessive; she sounded proud, like a wife bragging up her husband's good qualities. She was, Marty guessed, about fifteen, a runaway most likely, with her own scared and hungry days not far behind her; now she had a sort of family. She could be pleased because her man had a kind heart. Well, any family's better than none.

Thea was standing in the side yard when she got there, guarding their two boxes but not trying to carry them in. She lit up when she saw Marty. "I'd have taken some of this stuff in, but I don't know where you want it."

"In the kitchen. I get to use the stove and sink, as long as I don't get in the way." Marty lifted the larger of the boxes and started up the walk. "We'll give her something, it's only fair." Thea sorted out a few parcels and started after her, almost bumping into the lady of the house on the way in.

"Aunt Susan, this is my friend Thea — Thea —"

"Shuler," Thea filled in.

"She's going to stay for a few days, if you don't mind. Just till her job comes through."

"She's lucky to have a job coming," Aunt Susan said mournfully. She was a sad-looking woman anyway, her mouth turned down and her hair skinned back in a discouraged-looking home permanent, but she didn't look unkind. "I see that riffraff next door gave you a lift."

19

Marty said carefully, "I think they look worse than they are. They're noisy, but they act all right." She began unpacking her loot, setting aside a can of peas, a packet of powdered milk, a box of cornmeal. "We want you to have a little something out of this. After all, you're doing me a favor, letting me stay here."

Both cartons on the kitchen table, she sorted everything out while Thea shelved it. Tomatoes, two cans of pork and beans, a can of sweet potatoes, more powdered milk, dry pinto beans, rice, two bars of Ivory soap, oatmeal, cornmeal, a dozen eggs, dried prunes — Thea went back and forth, to and from the pantry, as if hypnotized. Aunt Susan sagged against the kitchen table watching her, suspiciously at first and then with a more friendly expression. Anyone could see she was a nice girl, would have been pretty enough to get by if it hadn't been for the smaller arm and leg. She had always looked at Marty with a feeling of unease; Marty was too big, too solid, too — well, unfeminine. (The word is dykey, Marty thought, tracing the change of expression across Aunt Susan's face.) This younger one looked like a nice girl.

There was a box of pancake mix, a small jar of honey, a loaf of white bread, a small bottle of dish detergent and a can of chili. Thea carried the chili back to the kitchen. "Could we have this for lunch?"

Marty would have started with oatmeal; chili pepper was likely to be a blow to stomachs that had been empty for awhile. But if that was what Thea wanted — "I don't see why not."

"You can use the kitchen now, if you've a mind

to." No one would have guessed from Aunt Susan's flat tone that it was ten in the morning, neither breakfast nor lunch time. She put away her own share of the loot and vanished into the front of the house, where beds were waiting to be made and bathtubs cleaned. "Goodness knows I'd like to do something for you if I could," she told them from the closing doorway.

"You've done a whole lot for me." Marty found the can opener and a saucepan. Alone with Thea, she said, "We can go out and look for throwaways later, but let's take a nap after we eat. I don't think either of us slept much last night — too hot. Unwrap the bread and get down a couple of bowls, will you?"

Fifteen minutes later Thea dropped her spoon in the sink, looking disappointed. "It's funny. I was hungry enough to eat an elephant, and I don't even have room for one bowl of chili."

"People's stomachs shrink. The trouble is, they don't shrink on the outside. I wouldn't be thin if I hadn't eaten for a year."

"You wouldn't be alive, either." Thea ran water over the two bowls, two spoons and pan. She had figured out that Aunt Susan wanted her kitchen tidy at all times. It was a dark, plain little room, with none of the gadgets housekeepers are always buying — no plastic clocks shaped like frying pans, no cute plaques or flowered curtains. But it was spotless. She asked restlessly, "What do we do now?"

"Rest for a while, I guess."

"I don't feel like sleeping."

"We can't go back to the food stamp place

21

because we don't have any bus fare. I can panhandle for it, but this isn't a very good neighborhood — but I will if you want."

Thea shut her eyes. "Maybe if we wait a day or two I'll get used to the idea."

"Won't do any good. Reaganomics — taking all the money out of the entitlement programs and feeding it to the murder machine." Marty leaned against the sink, considering. "There's a kind of a little park at the end of the block. Not fancy, but it has a couple of mulberry trees. We could read for a while, or take a nap."

"Sounds all right." Thea didn't want to spend the afternoon cooped up in Marty's hot little bedroom, with no fan or swamp cooler. "It must be a hundred in the shade."

"There'll be a breeze. One thing about Tucson, there's always a breeze, even when it's a hundred and ten. Now in Phoenix you can melt any time." It was obvious that Marty had lined herself up in the rivalry between the cities. "Must be all the hot air from the legislature. You got anything to read?"

"Two paperbacks from the library. Do you like historical novels?"

"Depends. I had a library card, but they billed me for a book they thought I lost, so I haven't gone for a while."

Park was an overstatement. It was really an empty lot with a diagonal path where people had taken a shortcut. But there were two trees and a few straggly flowers in an oblong bed. Marty spread out the jacket she had brought, after inspecting the sandy earth and clumps of bermuda grass. "You have to

22

watch out for ants. I got into a nest of fire ants once — man, I didn't sleep for two nights." She settled down, head bent, arms wrapped around her knees. "It's nice and quiet out here." Her tone didn't encourage talk.

Thea stared away into the distance, although there wasn't anything to see except the house across the street and a few passing cars. After a moment she shut her eyes against the glare. Sunglasses, she thought. Could I steal a pair? She had never stolen anything, the thought made her stomach feel funny, but in her mind's eye she could see herself, very small and clear, in a supermarket, her hand darting out to seize a pair of dark glasses from one of those revolving racks; herself sauntering out looking cool and calm. It struck her that it was practically impossible to be honest if you didn't have any money. You had to lie to get on welfare, you had to steal if you couldn't buy what you needed. She said out loud, "Tampons."

"Hmmmm?"

"How do you get stuff like that?"

"Swipe a package when the clerk isn't looking. Some people tear up the sheets, but I couldn't do that to Aunt Susan."

Now that Thea's mind had started to travel along this track, it kept going. "What happens if we get sick?"

Marty said airily, "We either die or get well." The look on Thea's face was too much; she added quickly, "If you're real sick, like a heart attack or a broken leg, they rush you to the hospital in an ambulance. The care is okay, I guess. If they think you're bad enough off they book you in — indigent. There's a county hospital, but it really isn't for poor people anymore, you have to pay if you possibly can."

"I had insurance when I was at the university."

"You were at the university?"

"I had a grant, but it ran out. I couldn't find a job, or anything. People look at my leg," Thea said bitterly, "and figure there's something wrong with my head. I got good grades, too."

"I bet you did."

They were silent for a moment. The air hummed with insect sounds and the whoosh of tires from the street.

Marty said, "We won't be broke forever. One of us will get a job. I generally have one — I worked with a landscaper for a while — that was neat — and if I could have found a ride I might have gone back to Circle K. There aren't any buses at night." She swallowed hard. She hadn't forgotten the terror of that holdup, the screams, the blood on the floor, the look on Paco's face as he crumpled down, and the cold terror of knowing she would be next. She said with phony cheerfulness, "All we have to do is hang on."

Thea didn't look convinced.

"Look," Marty said in exasperation, "we're young and single and healthy, no kids to worry about. You do know that thousands of kids are coming home from school to empty apartments every day, don't you? Either their mothers don't earn enough for day care or else there just isn't any day care to begin with. The feds have cut down on funding, and you won't find the right-to-lifers worrying about anybody

24

who's already been born. Anyhow," she got herself back on the track with a little effort, "we're young and more or less educated, and we're Anglo. You might not have noticed — you did say you're from Jersey —"

"My mother's Jewish," Thea said simply. "There's a lot of anti-semitism where I came from."

"Here it's the native Americans and the Chicanos. The Chicanos have a good family system and the Indians get part of whatever the tribe has, which is mostly hunger and unemployment. It's still a white man's world out here in the desert. You can put the accent on *man*, too." Marty stopped; she was getting into deeper water than she had meant to. "And we're fairly smart. There's a lot of mental patients around, a lot of retardees — you see them digging stuff out of the garbage cans. You and me, we have all our marbles. We'll get along."

And we have each other, she thought; at least it looks that way. Twenty-four hours ago she didn't know this kid existed, and here she was talking to her like they were sisters, or buddies. Kind of nice. Anyhow we're sharing a bed and a lot of free food. She said softly, "Althea Shuler."

"I don't know your last name."

"Brown. Plain old Martha Brown."

"I like it."

Yeah, and you'll like me till you find out what I am, Marty thought. That's tomorrow's problem. I'll worry about it tomorrow, like Scarlett O'Hara.

She didn't feel like reading, and anyway the sun was too bright. She shut her eyes and tried to relax, lowering her sweaty forehead to her knees. Rest when you can. You never know what's going to happen next. Maybe she'd get a job and work her ass off for legal minimum, or less. That's if she was lucky.

She knew Thea was looking at her. Even with her eyes shut, she wasn't going to get any rest there. She could hear the kid's mind going around. She sighed. "You're really worried, aren't you? Okay, we'll go and sign up at the state employment agency. Not that it'll do any good. They hardly ever have any jobs. But if it makes you feel better —"

Thea brightened, but she didn't stand up. "It's clear across town. We don't have any money for the bus."

Alone, Marty might have hitchhiked. She had done it many times and never came to any harm — of course, you had to pick your drivers. But she supposed Thea would be afraid to try. "We'll get some. Come on."

The six blocks to the neighborhood shopping plaza seemed to have stretched out since the last time she walked them. The plaza was a block long, recessed from the street, with plenty of parking space between the sidewalk and the covered arcade behind which the stores lined up: supermarket, drugstore, shoe store, hardware, branch bank, two fast-food places, dime store, gift shop. Marty took her stand in front of the supermarket. Shoppers coming out with loaded carts were apt to be aware of the high price of everything and likely to feel sympathetic to the down and out. She would have liked to let Thea do the asking, the kid was not only handicapped but small and puny-looking, but she was fairly sure Thea would have been scared to death at the idea. She wiped her forehead on her sleeve. "It's a bitch, isn't it? It'll go right on getting hotter till the sun goes down, too."

Thea said, "We need two dollars and forty cents."

"Soon as I can, I'm going downtown and get some low-income bus passes. If we get more than we need we'll have an iced tea, or something. There's nothing like a cold drink to make you feel better."

Thea looked unconvinced.

In spite of the weather and the hour — mid-afternoon, a time when people liked to take off their shoes and stay indoors — there was a good sprinkle of cars in the parking lot and a steady stream of people coming out of the grocery, pushing shopping carts. Most of the shoppers were Anglo; barrio housewives, with their little kids down for naps and the noon dishes washed, would be resting, or planning supper — before the day of swamp coolers and air conditioning, their mothers had arranged the afternoon around the siesta. The young couples coming out of the stores wore shorts and jogging shoes, looked hot and bad-tempered, and the old ladies walked as if their feet hurt. Marty stood under the covered arcade, not too close to the old Mexican who was trying to sell homemade tortillas or the skinny boy with the guitar, hopeful cap at his feet. The cap was empty, a bad sign. She waited until a plump old lady came along. "Ma'am, could you spare a little change? I need money for food."

The old lady glared. "Why don't you get a job? You look healthy enough. You ought to be ashamed, out here begging!" She didn't seem to connect Thea with this enterprise, and Thea stepped back a little, looking confused. She's about ready to run, Marty thought. She said, "Why don't you go inside where it's cool?"

Thea shook her head. She might not be any help, but she was going to stand by.

The next old lady was more generous. Marty thanked her for the quarter, which was probably Social Security money and ill-spared. Then two gay guys came along, loaded with deli, and gave her a dollar.

It was almost four o'clock by the time they had enough to get them to the employment agency and back. It would be closed by the time they got there. Thea was looking pale and strained, and Marty was dreading the walk home, even with a shelf of food waiting for them. She said, "Let's walk around to the back and see if they threw anything out, seeing we're here," but her heart was not in it and she wasn't surprised when all they found was a couple of smashed cardboard cartons. Nothing was there but the dumpster, big and square and slightly smelly, and she hadn't sunk to that kind of scavenging. Not yet. She'd whore before she ate garbage.

They walked home slowly, not thinking of anything to say.

Chapter 3

They never got to the employment agency. With the bus fare jingling in Thea's change purse, halfway home they passed a fast-food place with a dog-eared sign in the window: Employment Opportunity. "Some opportunity," Marty said. "Well, shall we?"

"They can't do worse than say no."

The manager, who looked too young and worried for the job, sat them down in a corner booth and brought them coffee. "Damn college kids, they quit as soon as exams are over." He looked angry, but they both recognized that as part of the act, of course a

29

girl got a little experience and started looking for an easier job, more pay, something with a future. Fast food was strictly temporary. All student jobs were temporary; why would anyone with a degree settle for broiling burgers and pouring coke?

The manager sloshed non-dairy creamer into his coffee, sizing them up, and spoke directly to Marty. "You want to try it? Legal pay, three thirty-five an hour, thirty hours a week. I wish I could use you both, but there's only one opening."

"Maybe later," Thea said bravely.

"Sure." He wasn't about to hire her, but it didn't hurt to be polite. He looked Marty up and down.

Not much to look at, she knew, but she could work circles around the pretty giggly kids who drifted in looking for work.

"Can you use a cash register?"

"Sure." She never had, but she could learn, couldn't she? Three thirty-five times thirty hours, that was something over ninety dollars a week. It sounded unlikely — still, she had done that well at Circle K, she had saved money on it. She walked out with no thought for her aching feet.

Thea had been doing arithmetic in her head. "That's a hundred dollars a week. And fifty cents."

"They'll take out for taxes and Social Security, twenty or maybe more, and I'll have to buy a uniform."

"It's still a lot. I'm glad for you."

"What do you mean, glad for *me?* I'm glad for both of us — while it lasts."

"I can't live on your money."

"What are you going to live on, then?" That was a dumb way to put it, as if the kid couldn't get along

30

without her. Marty was sorry as soon as the words were out of her mouth. She tried again. "Would you throw me out if you were the one that got the job? I thought we were partners even if you don't know me very well, even if you don't have any reason to trust me."

Thea's face reddened. "I mean, I'm already taking up half of your bed, I'm eating your food."

"It's as much your food as mine. You went after it too."

They stopped in the middle of the sidewalk, looking angrily at each other. Marty said, "Let's sit down on the bus bench. My feet are tired."

An old man was on the bench, smoking his pipe. He moved over, politely, so they could sit together. Marty bent to fasten the Velcro strips on her jogging shoes. "My feet swell in this weather. You notice they didn't say anything about fringe benefits. Like health insurance, or paid vacation. That's because nobody stays long enough to need them."

"Don't change the subject."

"All right. You know one person alone is out of luck. When you got a family, they all put in what they can. You get sick, there's somebody to take care of you. Like those kids next door — if one gets a food box, they all eat. If one has a joint, they pass it around. Probably wear each other's clothes. They're like a family, and I bet they never saw each other till they drifted into the neighborhood."

"But it's your money."

"I suppose if you got a job, you wouldn't share with me?"

"That's different. You're the kind people hire. They take one look at me and say no."

31

"You went to college for a while."

"A little over a year. Everybody goes to college, if they can get hold of the money. You don't have to be smart."

That was what Marty had always supposed; she couldn't contradict it. She said, "You could do something, teach school or work in an office. One of these days you'll find something, and me, I'll still be making Jumbos in a Burger Palace. Am I supposed to not let you do anything for me, or can I move into your big apartment with a swimming pool?"

Thea took a long, quivering breath. "All right, you talked me into it. We're partners."

Aunt Susan's kids were out in the yard when they got home — two boys and two girls ranging from about five to ten. "Kids, this is Thea. She's going to stay here for awhile."

They looked at her, not much interested. The younger boy asked, "What happened to your arm?"

Thea said, smiling, "A germ bit it. That's why you must be brave about having your polio shots." He recognized this for what it was, grownup preaching for his own good, and ignored it.

The boarder was in the bathroom. Aunt Susan was in the kitchen, fixing rice with something or other for supper. Marty put her head in and said, "I got a job at Burger Palace. Temporary, probably." But Aunt Susan went on slamming pots and pans around, without answering. Now she would have to offer some kind of token payment for the use of the room, which was fair enough. Still, if she'd had more sense she could have had the whole paycheck for herself, and saved something. But she would have felt guilty. Aunt Susan made every nickel do the work of a dime. Four kids need a lot of shoes even if you bought them secondhand. Besides, the inflow of cash would be connected in her mind with Thea's moving in, and would make her feel better about having the two of them in that hot little room.

They went out on the back steps, took off their shoes and let the slightly cooler air flow over their feet. A couple of the runaway girls came out next door with bags of garbage, and waved at them but didn't say anything. Marty said dreamily, "I'm thinking what we'll have for supper."

"Takes serious thought. We even have a choice."

Marty felt tired and let-down. Christ, she thought, I ought to be happy as a clam, seventy-five bucks coming in every week — as long as I last, and I bet I'll be their best worker as soon as I catch on to those fancy registers. I can keep my mind on the job, I won't be making up to the guys that come in. We can have new shoes, we can go down to Fourth Avenue and check out the resale shops. But the idea wasn't as exciting as it should have been.

I've adopted this kid, she thought. I never meant to do any such thing, I could have lent her part of my first week's pay and let her go off on her own, but no, I had to get all mushy and big-hearted and hand her a lot of talk about being a family. Like she'll have a job pretty soon. She may and she may not, how do I know? I had to talk first and think later. Now I'm stuck with her.

Suppose some night she decided to go to a bar, have a beer and check out the action? Marty had never been a bar person; in what she thought of as B-H, Before Hospital, she had been too scared and guilty to do anything but look at women on the street and wonder how they would be in bed. She would have dropped dead if one had spoken to her. She was all the terrible things Mom had yelled at her when she found out about Stan, only she was even worse because (Mom didn't know the worst of it) she liked women, not men.

Then there were the eight months in the psych ward, and Eileen. Funny, she couldn't remember what Eileen looked like. Just a glimpse now and then of the little pointed face under the white cap. She could remember the touch of Eileen's hands on her, though, touching her gently where no one else had, and the feeling that welled up and spilled over in her when she finally let it. Only three times, and then there were all those nights when she awoke in a ward full of sleeping patients and thought about Eileen and did for herself what she wanted Eileen to be doing for her. That made her feel guilty too — Mom had caught her doing it once when she was a little thing, not more than nine or ten, and slapped her hard and yelled at her. Maybe that was why she had never dared to tell Mom when the bad things started happening.

She hadn't made the connection at the time, but now, eleven years later, she supposed it was this attitude of Mom's that was really responsible for getting her into the psych hospital. She had grown up taking for granted that she was no good. There was never anyone she could tell about the things Dad did to her, but she recognized vaguely that they had some connection with the things Mom had caught her doing to herself, and the whole shebang was tied together somehow. It was dirty, all of it.

She was sixteen when she quit school and went to

work, assembly line work at the spark-plug factory. She didn't make friends there, the girls were all crazy about boys and clothes, and the guys wanted to get their hands on anything female — not for her, she had had enough of that. But the money was wonderful. She knew now that it wasn't really that much, but at first she had gone wild over spending. She bought record albums and a turntable, good shoes — she'd gone through childhood in secondhand shoes that never fit quite right — and meals in restaurants. Then, when the payment on her charge account came due she kited her paycheck, and of course she did it clumsily and got caught. The store manager called the cops.

By pure luck, she pulled a public defender who was young, full of ideals and not too happy with the legal system of which he was supposed to be a part. When he found that she was only seventeen, he persuaded the judge to order some psychiatric care for her instead of remanding her to Juvenile. So there she was in County, criminal but theoretically crazy, for passing a bad check. And there was Eileen, like a miracle.

She didn't remember the psychiatrist at all, though it was his report that had sprung her. It was Eileen who had cured her, making her see that it was all right to be what she was — what they both were. That was a secret she had hugged to herself for almost three years now, because she couldn't have explained even if she had known anyone to share it with.

On her own in Seattle, with a lousy job in a TV shop, she had ventured into a couple of lesbian bars. Both were decent places, she guessed, but she sat by herself, scared that someone would speak to her. It wasn't much of a record for an admitted, self-recognized dyke over thirty, with what was probably a normal sex drive.

Suppose she got brave enough to look for someone? Suppose one of those pretty girls at the burger joint was gay, disguised behind makeup and earrings, and recognized her. What would she do, bring her home? Aside from Aunt Susan (and she wasn't going to stay here forever, as soon as she saved up a little she would find a nice furnished room somewhere), there was this scared kid in her single bed. She could see the look on Thea's face if she found out.

Well, she was stuck with Thea. Trapped by her own tongue. She would have to take it one day at a time, wait and see what happened, how it worked out. Maybe if she liked somebody else enough, she wouldn't mind hurting Thea's feelings.

The light in the kitchen went out. That meant Aunt Susan had put some kind of a meal on the dining room table and gathered her kids around it. The boarder, a nice older man who brought ice cream home on payday, would be out of the bathroom. She rushed up the back stairs, followed by Thea, who waited politely in the hall until she was through. "We've got all kinds of food. What would you like for supper?"

"Not rice. We'll have rice for breakfast."

"Could we have eggs?"

"Sure. Boiled, fried or scrambled?"

"Boiled. I know how to cook eggs so they're not hard or soft, but in between."

Marty managed a smile. "If we had some ham we'd have some ham and eggs —"

"— If we had some eggs. But we do."

The eggs tasted good. Two apiece, and Marty hadn't had an egg for a long time. She alternated it with bites of bread, enjoying the meal in an absentminded way. She was tired — no wonder, all the walking they had done, to the plaza and back. Maybe that was all that ailed her, tiredness, and the letdown of having some good luck for a change. Later she sat on the edge of the bed and tried not to think about anything while Thea had a quick shower, then carried her own sleeping clothes, panties and tee shirt into the bathroom.

Climbing into bed, while Thea moved over to make room for her, she said, "When I get paid we'll go to the laundromat. Everything I own is dirty."

"Mmmm."

Thea was asleep, with her belly full of eggs and bread and her head on Aunt Susan's lumpy pillow. She trusts me, Marty thought, she figures I meant what I said. She felt unhappy lying there with the car lights moving across the wall and the sound of an ambulance siren in her ears. It looked like she was never going to be free, never have any life of her own.

Chapter 4

It was hot in Burger Palace, even with the swamp coolers and kitchen fans going full blast. The big neon-lighted room with the yellow plastic booths and little orange tables where the customers lingered over their Jumbos, fries and Coke were cool, but the open kitchen behind the order counter fairly sizzled with heat. Jake took Marty off her register around eleven, long before the school kids and street crew piled in, and sent his favorite blonde to replace her. "You see to the fries and slaw, kid. You're my fastest worker."

When the rush let up she could fix herself a tray

— burger and fries and a cold drink — and carry it to the front booth, which was reserved for staff when customers didn't need it. When things got too thick and fast, breaks were cancelled.

She slid a paper of fries onto a little plastic tray, added a cup of slaw, and handed it to the burger chef. Payday today, her second — it was her third week on the job, but checks were held back for a week. She was starting to think about opening a checking account, if there was anything left by the time she and Thea finished shopping. She had bought a pair of sneakers to wear on the vinyl-covered floors, and of course the uniform had taken a bit out of her first paycheck, but otherwise they hadn't bought a thing except food. She figured she was coming out about eighty dollars ahead, enough to outfit them both and still leave something over. The thought gave her a nice rich feeling.

Orders were coming in fast. She carried two loaded trays to the counter and got a smile from the girl who was filling cups. The truth was she liked seeing the customers, liked taking care of them, especially the old couples on Social Security who treated themselves to a meal out when the check came in, and the retarded folks from the Section Eight building across the street. Some of the retardates looked odd, but they were polite and grateful for a friendly greeting. She guessed they were doing the best they could with what they had, and that was more than you could say for some people.

She liked the kids, too. Their language was outrageous, especially when half a dozen fourteen-year-olds crowded into a booth, acting macho, trying to impress the girls at the next table, but they would mellow some as they got older. Let them have a good time while they were young. If they got too noisy or started punching each other, Jake would ask them to leave. But that didn't happen very often.

The two young fellows who ran the rubber-stamp place came in together, as they did three or four times a week, ordered Jumbos and coffee, and carried their tray to a small table at the back. They weren't much older than the high school kids, but they had a sober responsible look — roommates who were trying to make a go of their little independent business. She had seen them several times at the Lo-Price, pushing their cart and choosing their groceries. She liked to see them so pleased with each other's company, with so much to talk about; she hoped that everything would work out for them and they would stay together a long time.

She wished she had someone to go home to. Not Thea, who was a nice kid and good company but no part of any future she could imagine; she wanted someone who would fall into her arms when she opened the door, and lead her to the bedroom — someone who would plan for new furniture and help with the Saturday cleaning. Marty had hated housework when she was a child, but she could see herself walking home with a steak for supper and maybe painting the walls in an apartment of her own. None of that old femme-butch shit — thank goodness that was all over before her time — but she could see making a home with someone, watching TV after supper and maybe having a few friends in on Sunday evening.

She realized, surprised, that she had never made love in a bed. Never really made love at all. With

Eileen there had been little bits of time snatched from real life and her status as a patient — no privacy, no sense of security behind a locked door. What would it be like to have a home, a bed with a mattress and smooth sheets?

Jake was looking at her. Her hands were slowing down while her mind daydreamed. Peg said, "Hey, wake up, the customers are waiting." She started scooping fries, on the double.

Having Thea around was all right. She was quiet, but she knew a lot of interesting things, and now that she had a library card she was always coming up with little bits from the historical novels she liked to read. She washed the breakfast dishes and put them away, now that Marty was working from seven to one. Thea was the one who decided that they should keep on getting the food boxes, since the church ladies didn't ask any questions and no one knew how long a job would last. She went with the next-door kids and picked up their stuff, the skinny boy — Larry — helping with the carrying. She made the employment office every week; they never had a job for her and most likely never would, but she kept trying. Someone on the bus had told her about a place that found temporary jobs for people, and Marty had urged her to go there and register. If they came up with something, even if it was only one day a week, she would have it made.

It was kind of like having a younger sister around. But what did you do with a younger sister if you found a lover? Not that there was much chance of that.

Where do you find someone when you're thirty and not sure of anything?

41

"Marty, stop goofing off!" Jake sounded irritated, and she didn't blame him. He wasn't paying her to moon around over imaginary lovers.

She stopped at the bank on the way home — it was sure handy having everything right here in the neighborhood — and cashed her check. Aunt Susan was sweeping the front porch when she got home. Waiting for her ten bucks — you couldn't blame her, having money come in when you needed it was like taking a drink of cold water when you were thirsty. It wasn't anything but a token payment — Marty would have liked to give her more, but she had a dependent of her own to think about. They said a few words about the heat and then Marty went upstairs, knowing that Thea would have heard them and was expecting her.

What she didn't expect was that Thea would be lying limply across the bed, in bra and panties, bare feet dangling. She looked up listlessly when Marty came in.

"What's the matter, kid? You feel sick?"

"Just the curse. I used all your tampons."

"Do you have cramps, or anything?"

"No, I just feel depressed. I can't go on living off you, it makes me feel so ashamed."

"No reason it should. Look, I'm going to give you a little money so you can buy stuff you need — you know. You'll feel better with a little change in your pocket." She separated two ones from the wad in her pocket and added a third, put the bills in Thea's hand and curled her fingers around them. "When you get a good job you can put a little extra in the kitty, okay?"

Damn! There she went again, acting as if they

42

had some kind of a lifetime contract. If Thea ever got a good job, which wasn't likely, she could go off somewhere and live her own life, more power to her. She, Marty, wasn't going to be a nursemaid. It was too late to take anything back, better drop it for now. "Come on, get your clothes on. We're going shopping."

Thea rolled off the bed and headed for the bathroom. "I don't want you to buy anything for me. I'll go along and look, though. I like to window shop."

"Depends what we find. Might be a whole outfit, might be nothing at all. We ought to go every week, that's how you pick up the bargains."

They took the bus, transferred in front of a gas station where there was no bench, much less one with a ramada, and rode in silence past the university buildings to Fourth Avenue, Tucson's answer to Greenwich Village. Stores selling futons, incense, costume jewelry, recycled clothes from the Twenties and Thirties, candles, posters, new and used books. Used everything, in fact. It looked as if every charitable enterprise in town had a resale store here, from the Sallies to the high-class private schools. Thea looked dazed. "Where do we start?"

"With the closest one."

At the Salvation Army they picked their way past fairly good-looking davenports — there was one in earth-tone stripes that Marty would have bought if she'd had a place to put it — shelves of books, boxes of tangled jewelry, unmatched plates and glasses, electric irons that needed a little fixing, racks of clothes. "Look at this. Only a dollar and a quarter, and it has to be size five!"

43

Thea's eyes and mind were not on dresses. "Do you mind if I buy a book?"

"Hell, it's your money. Spend it however you want."

Marty examined the shirts, held shorts against herself, gave a passing glance at a pink evening dress with sequins, looked at and rejected some well-worn loafers, and inspected a crock pot. Thea came to join her, carrying two paperbacks — a quarter apiece, how could she resist them — and they sauntered on down the street, past the food co-op, past restaurants with cute names.

"You hungry, kid?"

"Sort of. I didn't feel like eating this noon."

"Now that was dumb of you," Marty stopped in the middle of the sidewalk, almost colliding with a knobby-kneed bearded boy carrying a guitar. "I didn't eat either, too busy. Let's stop in the Dairy Queen and get a cone to tide us over." She considered. "We'll eat someplace before we go home. Someplace cheap, but not hamburger. I do love to eat out."

They chose butter pecan, medium, and walked along licking cones, trying to keep ahead of the melt.

Thea laughed. "A month ago I'd have sold my soul for a hamburger, and you're being snooty about them."

"Comes from dishing them out all day. Here's Value Valley, it's the best of all. We can't take our cones in, though."

Cones finished with sticky hands wiped down pantlegs, they went in. Marty put in an afterthought. "Shows how fast you get used to being rich. Nobody ever offered me a nickel for my soul anyhow."

"Mephistopheles, coming up in a cloud of sulfur

and brimstone," Thea suggested. "There's no market for souls. All the politicians are giving them away."

Value Valley was busy. Girls in twos and threes, old ladies hanging onto their pocketbooks, plump Mexican mothers with two or three little kids trailing along, nervous-looking Anglos with their kids running up and down the aisles, old men who looked as if nobody took care of them — everybody was looking for bargains. It was Friday, payday, and it was also the second of the month — welfare checks were in. Marty headed for a rack of slacks marked "Small."

Thea said, "Hey, you take a medium at least."

"I'm looking for you. There's always a lot of good smalls. Living on starch plumps a person up."

An old man sitting on a wooden box appealed to Thea. "How do these look?" he had one tired sneaker on, the other lying on the floor beside his shoe.

"Looks neat. How does it feel?"

"Pretty good. And it'll wash."

Thea nodded. "Try on the other one. Sometimes one fits and the other doesn't."

Now, she's not shy with that old geezer, Marty thought. Why? Because he's worse off than she is? She's still young? Because she can help him? Maybe she ought to ask Thea for advice, or something. She turned away and started going methodically through a box of panties, brand new, store surplus, marked at twenty cents.

They came out an hour and a half later loaded with packages. Four pairs of shorts, wearable almost all year round in this climate, two pairs of jeans, quite a few tee shirts and a pair of shoes apiece — loafers for Thea, moccasins for Marty. The woman at the checkout counter had stuffed everything in two

45

big paper bags, one labeled *Goldwater's* and one *J.C. Penney*. Plainly the resale shops recycled their bags as well as their clothes.

Marty felt a little bemused after searching through so many racks and discarding so many near misses. She said smugly, "We did pretty good, don't you think?"

"I feel like Princess Di."

"Let's get something to eat. You like tacos?"

"I don't know. I never ate one."

Marty stared. "Practically straddling the border, and you never ate a taco? Next thing you're going to tell me you never ate a chimichanga or a flauta."

"I never did, either."

"We're going to Rosita's. What do college kids eat, anyhow?"

Thea grinned. "Hamburger."

Rosita's was small, cool and not as fancy as McDonald's; the people sitting around didn't seem to be in a hurry to leave. Marty had a chili relleno and a cup of coffee. Thea, torn, had a chicken taco and one with beef. Everything came with rice and refried beans, whether you ordered them or not. The whole thing came to a little over four dollars and they left feeling full and pleasantly extravagant.

"My tongue's burning," Thea said. "But it was worth it. I'll take you out when I get a job."

"That's a deal."

"Do you realize we had rice and beans, just like at home only better?"

"I'll get some chilis, if that's your idea of better. Everybody eats rice and beans. The Mexicans invented them."

"Does you good to do something you can't afford,

46

once in a while. When I get a job I'll take you somewhere elegant. With dessert."

Sure you will, Marty thought. People are sleeping in the park and begging for handouts, and you're going to get a swell job and eat at Janos'. She said, "I'll take two desserts, with whipped cream."

"You don't believe me," Thea said, looking stubborn, "but I will get a job. They aren't allowed to discriminate against handicapped people any more. It's like being black, or gay — or a woman."

"Yeah, rights look good on paper but nobody pays any attention to them in real life."

They were saved from quarreling by the arrival of the bus. Climbing on was quite a deal, with those big lumpy packages, but the driver waited while they set the stuff down and found change for the fares. "Been shopping?"

"You bet." Marty would have liked to show off their bargains, but he started up with a roar of the motor and she figured she had better let him keep his mind on his driving.

It wasn't until they were almost asleep that Thea roused up to say, "The Mexicans did *not* invent rice. Marco Polo found it in China when he travelled there, and brought it back to Italy."

"Well, it sure got around."

She was always amazed by the things the kid had come across in her reading. It was sort of nice having her around. Not enough, not love's young dream, but she had to admit it was something.

Chapter 5

By pure good luck, Marty was able to go to the
welfare office when Thea applied for the eighth or
ninth time. Jake switched everyone's hours around,
changed Babette's schedule so she could leave at one;
when he did, everyone knew they were sleeping
together. Babette sauntered out when Jake did, with
her hand through his elbow and a smug look on her
pretty face, and got into his car — but what the hell,
that was their business and who cared?

Now he shunted Marty over into mid-afternoon so
she could, unofficially, take his place when he was

gone. "You know, keep an eye on things. You're my best worker, kid."

"Flattery will get you everything," Marty said automatically. She sure wasn't going to tell anyone what to do, she wasn't a boss, but it was true that she would keep an eye on the kitchen and see that waiting customers got served. She missed the early morning cool and the feeling of having finished her day's work and being free, but now it was paying off. She dropped into a chair beside Thea and looked around. Welfare looked like DES, except that the molded plastic chairs were tan and the green walls were even grimier. There were only two people behind the semi-partition: a tall black man dressed fit to kill — who wore a white shirt and tie in this climate, in summer? — and a fat fair-haired woman with a little pursy mouth. But voices from behind the partition suggested that people were getting interviewed in the back room.

Thea, warned by experience that the wait would be long, had brought a book, but nobody else was reading and she must have felt that it would be improper, or maybe discourteous since she had someone with her. She sat with the book in her hand, looking blank. Marty looked at her from time to time, but couldn't imagine what she was thinking. She had begun to feel nervous herself, checked her pocket for pens and change and tissues, looked down at her knees, looked around at the half-dozen other silent applicants. She felt dimly that it was unfair for her to have a job, even if it was no position, when all these other people had to humiliate themselves by appealing for help. She was stronger than Thea, she should have been the one to fill out those forms and answer the humiliating questions. How did she get off having a regular job — no position, but still a job with a paycheck attached to it? She looked apologetically at Thea, who didn't return the look.

"Althea Shuler." Not such a long wait after all, but long enough to make an applicant nervous. Probably planned that way. Thea got up, stooped defensively, limping more than usual, and moved to the front of the room.

How did they decide who got a check, who was turned down? Computers, she supposed, but there had to be people to program them. Did it make a difference if the guy's breakfast was sitting right, if he had had a fight with his wife? Marty didn't like computers much, but she wished the decisions could be done by some kind of machinery, not strained through the prejudices of a human being.

The tall black man said something she couldn't hear, and Thea nodded, looking less scared. He was jotting down notes on one of those long printed forms, now and then stopping to check her answers against the sheets she had already filled out. He looked bored, not unkind but not interested either. Did this all day, five days a week, and she supposed you stopped looking at people after the first few hundred. It was like making Jumbos, so much ground beef, so much lettuce and tomato, so much onion; some wanted mayonnaise and some didn't. But people were not sandwiches, even if they looked that way when she was behind the counter.

She was sitting on the edge of the chair. She took a deep breath and made herself relax.

Thea, dismissed, vanished behind the door to the side of the interviewer's pen.

It was forever — it was fifteen minutes by the electric clock on the wall when she came out again, looking wilted and relieved, and stood waiting for Marty to join her. Probably they had it all figured out. Fifteen minutes for each applicant, to find out if she (there were always more women than men in the waiting room) deserved rent money and a food allowance, and medical care in real emergencies.

Marty took a deep breath as they came out onto the sidewalk. "Was it bad?"

"Not really." Thea had been sweating in spite of the air conditioning; her hair was stuck to her forehead. "They're supposed to let me know."

Marty waited for the green light. "This town is full of crazy drivers." The light changed; she waited a moment to be sure that the crazy drivers were actually going to stop, and they crossed.

"Reagan says there's a safety net under the poor, but it sure has a lot of holes in it."

"At least they don't send a case worker around to snoop into your private life, like they used to. They do their snooping in the office, by appointment."

"I'd still rather have a job," Thea said tiredly.

They sat down on the bus bench. Thea closed her eyes against the glare. Marty said, "You still need dark glasses."

"I don't want you spending money on me."

"It's cheaper than a Seeing Eye dog."

"No, they're free."

What could she do about a girl who knew all the answers?

A solid old woman appeared out of nowhere and bent to fumble through the city waste bin in its concrete shell. She came upright with a crumpled newspaper and a soft drink can, looked suspiciously at the two younger women, and picked up a couple of cigarette butts from the sidewalk. She moved away slowly. Her feet were swollen and wrinkled; she walked as though they hurt.

Marty said, "I haven't seen anybody sniping butts since I used to eat in a rescue mission."

"She's going to put those things in her mouth?"

"She'll take them apart and put the tobacco in a piece of toilet paper."

The old woman was halfway down the block. Thea said timidly, "I wish we could give her something."

"There's millions of her."

"Yesterday when I went to the library there was a boy asleep under a tree, with his backpack under his head . . ."

"Millions of him too. We're lucky we have a place to sleep. 'Specially when the monsoon season comes on."

The bus slowed and stopped. They got on. Marty said, "Let's stop at the Dairy Queen for a cone. It's so hot."

They chose vanilla, being cooler than chocolate. "In Jersey," Thea said, "it gets hottest around noon and then it starts cooling off. Here in the desert it just keeps getting hotter till the sun goes down. Have you noticed?"

"I've noticed, all right."

Thea wasn't through with poverty. The *really* poor, she might have said, who didn't have food boxes or a cousin with a spare bedroom. When she got hold of an idea she worried it like a dog with a bone.

"The TV says unemployment went down two percent last month."

"That means the number of people on comp went down two percent. Every month a lot of people use up all their benefits and drop out of the statistics. They don't exist as far as the government is concerned."

"How do they manage?"

"Any way they can. Like us."

Thea looked at her cone as if maybe she had no right to it, though they had bought the smallest size. "The woman I talked to, back there, she said you can't get on welfare unless you have a permanent address. What do the rest do?"

What would you have done if I hadn't come along? Marty thought. Starve, or beg, or go on the streets. Steal stuff, or mug old ladies, or eat out of dumpsters. She said, "I know it's not fair, but let's not talk about it. Don't do any good to lie awake nights, worrying. Leave it to the do-gooders, and young radicals, and college professors. I don't know the answers."

Thea walked along, thinking it over. Well, hell, Marty thought, I'd worry about it too if I had time. She wiped her hands down the side of her shorts. "You know the difference between you and me? You worry over stuff until you come up with some kind of an answer, and I pop off and then worry. That's because you're smarter than me."

"That's not so."

"Yes, it's smart to think things out. You know all kinds of things I don't. Like about ancient Greece —

I never knew any of that before, about the Sophists and all. That's really interesting."

"I got it out of a book," Thea said. "That's all I've had to do lately, read. While you were out earning the living."

Marty noticed that she said *the* living, as though they were really a family. Her own fault. She had been so concerned for the kid's self-respect that she kept harping on what's-mine-is-ours. She said, "You'll get a job or something one of these days. Look, what shall we fix for lunch? Something fast. I have to get to work."

Without saying so, they were both taking for granted that nothing would come of the interview. Thea had applied before and been turned down; she went back out of stubbornness. You applied for everything and hoped that now and then, out of freaky good luck, something would come through. Marty wouldn't have been surprised if the church people had suddenly turned them down for food boxes, although she gave churches credit for being more humane than any government agency.

They went on their daily way, Marty reporting at Burger Palace in the heat of the afternoon, when tempers behind the counter were wearing thin, Thea filling in her time somehow, going to the library, giving Aunt Susan a hand with the laundry. She was reading a book a day and had branched out into history and travel stories; she talked with the runaway kids next door, did the wash in Aunt Susan's antique machine with the hand wringer, and had supper on the way to ready when Marty got home from work. Looks like we've got all the makings of a marriage except the most important one, Marty told herself. She's a nice little housewife.

They went to see *The Color Purple*. Thea's judgment being that it was good but too prettied up — the book was better. "You have to read the book. She knows how things really are."

"Sure." But she didn't read it; she was busy grilling hamburgers, dumping fries into sizzling fat, squirting Coke into paper cups and smiling at customers. When she got home she was tired. One reader in a family was enough. She even worked out a few comforting phrases for Thea when the welfare people turned her down.

They weren't needed, as it turned out. About twenty minutes to twelve on the day of Thea's second interview she walked into Burger Palace looking hot and sweaty but triumphant. She settled down in the back booth, and Marty ran two glasses of iced tea and carried them back, ignoring Jake's dirty look.

"Five minutes. I haven't had my break," Marty told him. He didn't look too happy about it, he liked to have the hired help lined up smiling and subservient before the noon rush started, but he let her get away with it.

"Fifty-five fifty a month for food," Thea said in a rush. "One-twenty for rent, that's 'cause I told them I shared an apartment, and thirteen twenty-three for clothes and stuff. How do you suppose they figured that out? Such a strange figure. Why not fourteen dollars? It'll take about a month for the first check to come through, Mrs. Gulick says, and if I run out of groceries they might advance a few dollars to tide me over. If I ever have to have an operation, or anything, they might pay my doctor bills. I can't believe it." She couldn't have been happier if she had inherited a million dollars.

"You're rich."

"We're rich. Now I can pay my share. Marty, can we look for a place to live? A little place, nothing fancy, with our own kitchen? Or a hot plate anyway?"

She really is a wife, Marty thought sourly. Only no love, no sex, no fun. How do I tell her to get lost? I'd like a woman in my bed, and not just for polite conversation.

Jake was looking at her. She patted Thea on the shoulder and scuttled back to the kitchen as five lanky boys with Mohawks shoved their way in and stampeded to a corner booth.

She didn't trust luck too far. They'd go on getting food boxes anyway, she decided.

Chapter 6

The neighborhood had been settled in Territorial days. The foot-thick adobe walls presented a solid front to the world. Thea, stumbling on the broken sidewalk, said, "I like it. It's like a village in Europe."

"You ever been in Europe?"

"I've seen pictures."

Larry said, "Come in and take a look. It don't look like much — don't expect anything fancy." He turned the key in the old wooden door and they followed him inside, hopeful and curious.

It was hard to tell how many rooms there were; they trailed into each other, without much in the way of partition. The kitchen end, where they entered, had a large water heater and some shelves, and someone had left a flower pot on the deeply recessed window sill. This area widened into a larger room with, again, a single wide window, and a door off that led into a sort of bathroom — no tub or shower, but a toilet with an overhead tank and a faucet dripping into a small basin. This was the only running water in the house; there was no sink in the kitchen. On the other side of the living area, the street side, a door led to what Marty supposed was meant to be a bedroom. This room had a sizable hole in the ceiling, through which the sky showed.

"How do you take a bath?" Thea wanted to know.

"Heat some water in the kitchen and carry it to the bathroom. There's a plug for the basin. Takes a little longer to wash your hair, but it can be done. Jeez, I've stayed in places where there wasn't even drinking water." Larry looked around. "The doors lock. The windows aren't busted. You even got a little back yard. What more could you want?"

"It looks sort of small."

"Empty rooms always do."

"Will the landlord fix the ceiling?"

"For a hundred a month he won't fix nothin'. Me and Juan will help you put a patch on it. You buy a sack of ready-mix plaster."

"Would we be safe here?"

"Depends. Nobody's going to murder you, or mug you. On the other hand, the druggies might bust in and steal your TV set."

Thea laughed. "We don't have a TV set. We don't have anything."

"Hell, you don't need much. Mattress, and a few dishes. The Starvation Army has great dishes. Course, they don't match, but who needs it?"

Marty said spunkily, "Long as we have food to put on them."

"By the way, I'm still doing food box pickup. Juan's brother has a car, sort of. You can go with us. It's easier than carrying stuff on the bus."

"We'll need something to cook on."

"There's no gas. I'll run a cord down from the light, with a double socket, and you can get a hot plate. We put a hot plate in the front room and an electric skillet in the bathroom — if you run 'em off the same outlet it blows every fuse in the place. There's no outlet in the kitchen, you'll need candles or a kerosene lamp."

A hole had been bored in the living room ceiling; a bulb dangled at the end of a long cord. Marty guessed that she could reach the switch but Thea probably couldn't. Maybe Larry or Juan — whoever he was — would get a longer wire and bring the bulb down.

"It's not the Doubletree, but you're not paying Doubletree prices. There's a bus line two blocks away. Lavenderia a block from that. You're in walking distance of Fourth Avenue. Co-op easy to get to. It's like Greenwich Village."

"You ever been to Greenwich Village?"

"Used to go down and look at it when I lived in New York. Edna St. Vincent Millay lived there, a long time ago. Mostly I hung around Forty-second Street. There weren't any jobs." He scanned their faces. Thea's was blank. Marty's showed a flash of comprehension. Larry went on quickly, "It gets cold there in the winter. The old winos sleep on sidewalk grates to keep from freezing. I decided I'd rather be broke and warm than broke and cold."

"You and a million others," Marty said. The City Council had been making a great to-do over transients; they funneled into the city from Chicago and Detroit and Hoboken and Seattle, Gary and Hackensack and all the Springfields, and someone had to feed them, but every time some charitable group tried to open a food kitchen the enraged neighbors petitioned to have it closed. "Those people" were a threat to decent citizens, they stole and murdered and raped and threw stones through windows (although no one had caught them doing any of those things). The City Council, on what statistical basis nobody knew, estimated that three thousand people were sleeping in their cars, having run out of gas to go elsewhere and money to stay in Tucson. Some had built a Reaganville of cardboard boxes and tar paper in the desert, carrying buckets of water in and cooking over campfires; it had been evacuated with fire hoses and tear gas bombs. You couldn't go into the blighted area that was Downtown without being panhandled, but the beggars, refused, walked away amiably enough. Marty reminded herself that she had begged bus fares in the very shopping plaza where she was now respectably employed.

Transients, she guessed, were just people who didn't have jobs and couldn't get on welfare. In a way, she and Thea were in that category, or had been, and she couldn't imagine either of them mugging anyone. She did draw a line between stealing from people, who probably needed their money, and stealing from organizations. She knew that some old people lifted a can of beans here, a chunk of cheese there when they ran out of Social Security money. She didn't blame them.

"You prejudiced about Mexicans?"

"No, why should I be?"

"People are funny," Larry said simply. "Around these neighborhoods they're mostly nicer than Anglos. All the old grandmothers mind the kids — you won't find any latchkey kids in the barrio. Somebody takes them in till the mama gets home from work. You'll like Juan."

"If you do, I do."

"We're an item." Larry looked out of the uncurtained front window, although there was nothing to be seen except the cracked and crumbling sidewalk and the whitewashed wall across the street.

"I'm glad for you."

"Me too," Larry said. "You'll like his mother. We're living next door to her. She says she has *tres hijos*, three sons — the other one is still at home. I not only got Juan, I got a mother-in-law too."

Marty glanced at Thea, who was looking polite and blank. She cleared her throat. "It'll be nice having you for a neighbor. How did you find this place?"

"Mama knows everything that's going on. I met Juan at the welfare office." For Larry, the oldest and most streetwise of the runaway kids, had achieved a welfare account of his own.

Marty could imagine the encounter, the sizing up: Is he? Yes, I think he is — the talk outside the door. She nodded.

61

"You think you want it?"

It was Thea who answered. "Sure."

"Then come and meet the landlord."

The landlord was short, fat, shrewd-looking, named Humberto — they never learned his other name. It was a sort of executive scrawl on the receipt he wrote out for their hundred dollars. Marty was left with about twenty dollars in her wallet — well, Thea's check would be in by the time they moved. They would be all right.

Kids on skateboards zoomed across the sidewalk in front of them. Little girls sat on a couple of porch chairs with their dolls. A tiny wrinkled old lady looked at them, curious but not unfriendly, as Larry walked them to the bus. Two pretty young women waved at him from the laundromat. Marty had never lived in a neighborhood like this — so many dark faces, so many pepper and palo verde trees, so many cats sunning on the sidewalk. It had a homelike feel. She said, "I'm going to like it."

"Like I said, it's no Doubletree."

"I picketed at the Doubletree once," Thea said. "That guy who was raising money for the Contras. A bunch of us from the U went. I was never inside, though."

Marty oriented herself quickly. Here was the mama-papa grocery with the hand-lettered sign in the window: "For a dime you can use their telephone." A string of chilis hung outside the door and she could see a bin of tortillas on the counter inside. Here was the bus stop. "Only five blocks to the food co-op. You're almost at Fourth Avenue when you get this far," Larry said.

Walking distance to the bead shop, the incense

shop, the radical Spanish bookstore, the women's bookstore, the place where furniture was refinished. And all the thrift shops. She had been on Fourth a hundred times, yet never knew these nice old-fashioned residential streets were so near.

Now if I don't lose my job, Marty thought, or Thea doesn't lose her welfare.

But she wasn't really worried. One good thing about being poor, she had found, was that you took one day at a time. If this month's rent was paid and there was food in the cupboard you didn't worry. Daydreams too were small ones — maybe next month they could buy a new tea kettle, or save out enough to go to the movies.

She didn't worry much about the rest of the world, though it kept pressing in on her. Actually, Thea was the only person she knew who really read the newspaper — somebody usually left one at Burger Palace and Marty folded it up and carried it home, but all she read was the funnies. What was more, Thea wanted to talk about the news. Would Nicaragua be invaded? What was going to happen in the Persian Gulf? How about this fight in the City Council? Thea was a worrier. She gave a dollar to the skinny boy asleep on the library grounds, backpack under his head, and then came home and talked about him. What did he eat? Did his family know where he was? What would happen to him when the nights got cold?

Marty had never gone hungry as a kid. No matter how miserable things were at home, there was always food on the table. And she doubted that Thea had. Home was no dream world, with Mom loaded half the time and the old man — but she wasn't going to

think about that. Like the shrink at the hospital said,
That was in the past, she wasn't guilty of anything
and her business was with the future, if she could
get her hands on enough money to live on — and
who knew? Maybe someday a beautiful woman would
come along and fall for her.

But wasn't it funny that Thea, with a year at the
university and her middle-class background, worried
so much about other people's troubles?

She said chattily as the bus rolled along, "I bet
we can get a mattress cheap at the Sallies. I've seen
them there. Or the Goodwill. We'll have to buy a
couple of sheets though, nobody ever gives away
sheets."

"J.C. Penney or Sears."

"Dishes and a hot plate, that's about all we
need."

"All the thrift stores have those bins full of
silverware."

"Towels, and something to put over the windows
so the neighbors can't see in."

Thea had been doing arithmetic in her head. She
was good at it. "You'll get paid Friday. My check
comes in on the first. That's only a week. Food boxes
a week from Thursday. On the twelfth the
government is giving away cheese. If Larry and Juan
go — maybe they don't know about it, we'll have to
tell them. I can stand in line if you're still on early
shift."

Jake had decided to put Marty back on breakfast
detail; he said the young ones came in half asleep
and goofed off all morning.

"Where did you find out about the cheese?"

"The kids next door. Word gets around."

The little wife, Marty thought, she'll go and stand in line while I earn the living. And she wished once again that she had somebody of her own, not a little wife exactly, but a woman who thought she was wonderful and came to bed panting to make love. When you're eating regularly you have time and energy to think about sex.

She was over thirty. Pretty soon she would be old. If she was ever going to find anybody, she better start looking. But how do you look for a lover when you're living with somebody who never heard of it?

As though she could read Marty's mind, Thea asked, "What did Larry mean when he said he and Juan were an item? That sounded funny."

Marty moistened her dry lips. "It means they're lovers."

"Oh."

"You do know guys can love each other, don't you?"

"Oh, sure. Women, too. I read a book called —"

"*The Well of Loneliness,*" Marty had to grin, shaky as her insides felt. "That's the one everybody reads."

Thea looked surprised. "No, *Beebo Brinker.* I didn't like her much — Beebo."

Marty couldn't think of a good answer. After a moment she said, "Most people aren't like Beebo. Most of them are like everybody else."

There was no more talk for a while. The subject was like a box of grenades; any one Marty picked up might explode.

They got off at the corner and went in to tell Aunt Susan she was losing her no-pay, lately promoted to low-pay roomers. They looked over what

65

was left from the last food box to fix for supper. Food was a good safe subject.

Marty asked, "Should we have eggs and plenty of bread, or string beans and ubiquitous rice? I thought I'd be sick of rice by this time, but the price is right."

She had skirted around it, she was safe. And there was the apartment to think about and plan for.

"Cindy says there's no food value in rice."

"For heaven's sake don't tell the Chinese, Japanese, Koreans, Thais, Filipinos — they've been living on it for years."

She wondered what Juan was like, and whether he and Larry would want to go into detail about their relationship. Guys did, sometimes. She would have to find some way to keep them from asking.

7

"I thought we were going to get along with just the hot plate."

Thea held the dented percolator tightly, as though someone were going to get it away from her. "It works fine. The lady at Goodwill plugged it in for me."

"But we drink instant."

"We can heat soup in it," Thea said patiently, "or cook vegetables. Or heat water for washing dishes. It's like having an extra burner."

She sounded so defensive Marty couldn't help smiling. "That's a point. I never thought about that."

Rico said, "Come on, come on, there won't be nothing left by the time we get there."

Juan looked over his shoulder. "Hi Thea. Hi Marty. Come on, let's go, the line will be a mile long already."

It was the twelfth of the month, federal surplus food distribution day. Their rent had started on the first, but they hadn't moved in until the ninth because Rico's beat-up Datsun was laid up for repairs. Even if you don't own anything but clothes and a few paperbacks, you need a car to move. During the waiting time, Larry and Juan had got hold of a sack of plaster and put a large bumpy patch on the bedroom ceiling. How long it would hold was anybody's guess, but it might keep out the worst of the rain.

"Get it on before the monsoon," Larry had said, embarrassed at being so helpful.

Marty said, "We owe you a meal," and meant it. As soon as she and Thea had a little something in the cupboard they would invite the three guys and Mama Ruiz over for supper.

Marty hoped they would help Thea if there was anything heavy to lift. She would liked to have gone along, but she was working from seven to one and it was after six now. She watched them drive away, then put on her orange apron and perky little cap and locked the door behind her.

It was nice and cool. Later the temperature would go up to 100, maybe more — last week it had been 107 — but now the air felt fresh and there was a good breeze. There was almost always a breeze off the desert; Marty guessed it had kept people alive and comfortable before electric fans and swamp coolers were invented. The thick adobe walls helped, too. And the bus was air-conditioned. The driver gave her a friendly look. "You still on the grill over there? I'll be over for a Jumbo around eleven, end of my run."

"I'll give you extra onion." It felt good to be part of the working world, to feel that people were friends even though she didn't know their names.

She and Jake almost collided at the door. She stood back while he unlocked, a boss's privilege, then went in and turned on the fans, checked out the cooler and started filling the paper napkin holders. There wasn't much to do, the night crew left things in order, but it made her feel important, almost as if she were a manger. She would never be a manager because she would never have money to buy a franchise, and anyway that wasn't what she wanted to do with her life, but it was fun to pretend.

The first truck driver came in for coffee, and she didn't have time to think about Thea and her secondhand coffeepot, or wonder how the others were making out, waiting in line for government cheese.

Thea was enjoying the morning cool too, the pleasure of going somewhere in a car and the company of Larry and Rico. She was almost sorry when they pulled up in front of the neighborhood house and she saw the block-long line in front of the concrete block building, the big truck from which huge cartons were being pulled.

"I guess this is it all right," Rico said, leading them to the end of the line. "Gonna take a while." It wasn't bothering him, he had all day, he had done

69

this before, but Thea felt tired just looking at all those patient waiting people.

There were old ladies with little camp stools, old men who somehow looked dirtier and shabbier than the women — no one to look after them, Thea figured, probably lived in furnished rooms and ate out of cans. There were young mothers with two or three little children hanging onto them and another on the way; the Pill takes money. Young men who might have had wives and children at home, girls with their hair up in plastic rollers, Hispanic, Anglo, Indian, Oriental. "O'Odham. Some Yaqui. The Navajo mostly take care of their own." Rico sized them up. All but the young children looked as if they had taken a beating from life.

The line inched ahead. Two men handed out cartons; people took them and moved away. Thea stayed close to Rico and Larry, as if they were family in a place where people might be unfriendly.

At Burger Palace, Marty took advantage of a lull to sit down with a cup of coffee and rest her feet. Like the others, she wore sneakers, but before the end of her shift her feet were hot and swollen. Regulations called for stockings, but no one paid any attention; nylons were like little hot packs after the first few minutes. "That's for back East," Babette explained.

By eight the sky was brassy and the heat came in whenever a newcomer opened the door. Marty hoped Thea was home with her loot, although Rico had predicted three hours' wait in line. She hoped there was some shade wherever Thea was waiting, although shade is a rare thing in Arizona. She hoped Larry and Rico would help her carry the heavy cartons. She

70

thought of Mrs. Ruiz, who would make lunch for them, and hoped that she would feed Thea too. The kid needed to be looked after.

Mama Ruiz had already adopted the two of them. She didn't speak more than twelve words of English, although Marty suspected that she understood a great deal; she communicated with pats and smiles, gifts of *pan dulce* and tortillas made by her sister in Nogales, *old* Nogales, on the other side of the border, the meal pounded in a *metate.* Some women are born to be matriarchs. Angelita Ruiz, mama and nana to the whole neighborhood, was one of them. Marty's Spanish was about as good as the old lady's English, but there was a pleasant feeling between them.

I'll make her something nice, she thought. If we had an oven — but there was no oven, anything she shared had to be cooked on a one-burner electric plate.

Business was good. Around ten the senior citizens began drifting in for coffee, a little interlude of cool and conversation. The retardates from the halfway house came in groups of four and five, self-consciously quiet and well-behaved, proving that they could manage on their own, counting out their money proudly — coping. Babette said she couldn't stand to look at them, but most of the counter girls made a point of being extra friendly. Kids came in for a paper of fries or a Coke, it was summer vacation and they had time to fill in, they didn't know what to do with themselves. Some of their mothers were working and anyway, who wants to hang around home? This is *vacation,* man. Life for most people slowed down in hot weather, but not if you made your living in fast foods. Leisure was for the customers.

71

A big truck pulled up just outside the door and the driver got out and stepped up to the sidewalk. She was about thirty, close to six feet tall, in neat tan pants and shirt and a cowboy hat, not uniform but not tourist-cute either. She carried a plastic thermos and swung a bunch of keys. Marty stepped up to take her order; Babette was in the john and Cindy was on break, no need to cut her off. "Two eggs over easy, bacon well done, fries and black coffee," the trucker said. "Will you fill my thermos with iced tea? Hundred and seven today, the TV says."

"You on a long haul?"

"Just down from Phoenix. It's hot there." The trucker took a paper napkin from the holder and wiped her forehead, pushing back the hat. "You new here? I haven't been in for a while."

"More or less." She could be brisk and businesslike too, but she couldn't size people up the way this woman was doing, as if she were in charge but friendly. Marty was conscious of brown eyes on her as she turned her back and broke eggs into the skillet.

That was how she would have liked to be: calm, confident, independent. Those slacks didn't come from Goodwill; the hat and boots were the kind you could wear forever, because they got smarter as they got older. She could see herself at the wheel of one of those big babies, maneuvering in and out of traffic on the Interstate, alert yet relaxed at the wheel. She had never driven a truck, but she bet she could learn.

She got everything on the tray, added napkins and creamer and two little packets of sugar, and handed it to the customer. "That looks good. You're fast, too."

"I hope the eggs are okay."

She was aware of the tall woman as she went back to the counter. She would remember her, watch for her to come in again. There were people who caught your eye if they only passed you on the street; this was one of them. She went back to the kitchen, where orders were piling up and tried to keep her mind on her work.

The truck driver finished her breakfast, came back for a second coffee and, on the way to the door, asked, "What's your name?"

"Marty."

She was out and gone, striding away as if she had something important to do but wasn't in any hurry. The truck pulled away. Everybody's dream dyke, Marty thought. Hell, she's probably married and has a couple of kids. It's nice to daydream, though.

When she started home a little after one, Jake stopped her. "You got a tip," he said, grinning. "That lady with the truck left you a dollar."

"You're kidding."

"Here you are. Just like waitressing at the Ritz." His tone was sarcastic. No one tipped in fast-food places.

"Thanks." She folded the bill and stuck it in her pocket. But Jake hadn't finished. "You got some special recipe for fried eggs?"

Marty eyed him. "Sure, an old family secret." She walked out, embarrassed and hot, but Jake's voice followed her. "You wanna watch out for that one. She's one of *those kind.*

She was angry all the way to the bus stop.

73

Who the hell did he think he was, putting down a woman like that? Marty's kind of woman. She knew it the minute she saw her get out of that truck, walking so smooth and easy. Who did that little twerp think he was?

She knows my name, but I don't know hers, Marty thought. Probably never see her again, anyhow.

She hadn't felt like this since the first time she caught Eileen looking at her across the rec room at the hospital. Across a crowded room, like the song says. Eileen didn't look anything like this woman; she was small and not so clean-cut, but the look was the same.

The adobe house was hot when she got home, but pleasantly dim after the dazzle outside. The glare always made her feel sick; she needed dark glasses. Thea was sitting by the kitchen table, a card table with a wad of paper under its one short leg. She shut her book but kept a finger in the place. "Look. Besides five pounds of cheese and two pounds of real butter, they're in the fridge."

There was a five-pound sack of flour, two pounds of cornmeal, two pounds of rice and a big jar of honey. "What are we going to do with all this flour?"

"Give it to Mama. She'll bake up something good."

Marty shoved it all into the refrigerator Mama had found for them, probably from one of her relatives. They were supposed to give her twenty dollars for it, if they ever had it. "Damn flour weevils," she said mechanically. "You can't leave anything out for a minute." The complaint was routine; she caught Thea's disappointed look and laughed. "It's wonderful, babe. I feel so rich."

All through supper — eggs scrambled with cheese in real butter — Thea reviewed the morning. The three-hour wait in the hot sun, the little old lady who looked as if she might pass out until Rico packed her and her groceries in the car and took her home — "Turns out she lives in the same street as his Aunt Emilia" — the neighborhood house itself. I got talking to a girl on the line, she goes there in the winter to swim. They have free Spanish lessons, too. We ought to go — you really need Spanish in Arizona."

"Sounds good, if you can figure a way to get there."

She thought she was doing all right, but by the time the last bite of egg was scraped off the plates Thea was looking at her curiously. "You sound tired. Did you have a bad day, or something?"

"I'm all right. You're the one that ought to be tired, standing out in all that sun."

Thea carried her coffeepot into the bathroom, filled it with water, carried it back to the kitchen and plugged it in. "You go to bed. I'll come as soon as I wash the dishes."

"I'll wash the dishes."

Thea stacked the skillet, two plates and two forks in the plastic dishpan. "No. I'll do it. You go on and get to sleep."

It was a long time before Marty slept, even after Thea came in and stretched out on her side of the mattress. Her mind wouldn't relax. She lay thinking about the tall truck driver and wondering if they would ever meet again. Not that anything interesting would happen if they did, of course.

Chapter 8

Babette was pregnant. It was the main topic at Burger Palace, getting more time and attention than the baseball scores, summer sales and record-breaking heat. Old ladies who came in on Social Security day let their coffee get cold while they offered advice and sympathy. Every time Jake, looking like a thundercloud, came near a knot of whispering girls the knot broke up and scattered. You didn't need two guesses to know what they were talking about.

Babette, wearing more eye makeup than ever, guessed that she was about three months along. The doctor said she was in good shape, no reason she couldn't have a healthy baby. She didn't look too good, there were circles under her eyes that never came out of a bottle and her skin was pasty, but of course pregnancy takes some women that way and the circumstances were far from ideal. The smell of hot grease in 105-degree weather sent her running to the washroom to vomit, and her parents were giving her a hard time. "My dad especially. Mom feels bad about it, but she's all right. My dad keeps yelling at me."

The baby was Jake's. Of course, Marty thought. Hadn't they gone off together, glittering with sexual excitement, almost every afternoon? Hadn't Jake come back to work looking as smug and satisfied as a tomcat? Nobody mentioned it, nobody ever came right out and asked, but everybody knew. Unless she had two men on the string at once, and she didn't seem like that kind of a girl. Babette's baby, due around the first of the year, was Jake's. They watched him. Even Mary Ann, who had only been working at Burger Palace for a couple of weeks, kept a cold eye on him. Women had to stick together in these things.

It was Mary Ann, though, who broke the silence. It was an accident, or maybe not altogether, because while Babette didn't come to work these days until noon, it was five minutes of and she would be there any moment. Mary Ann said, while Jake was in the john, "She's three months along. If she's going to get an abortion, she ought to do it. They'll set it up for her at Planned Parenthood."

And there was Babette in the doorway, looking tired but not angry or surprised. "I'm not getting an abortion. I'm having this kid."

"You're getting married?" Jean asked hopefully. "Invite us to the wedding."

"The son of a bitch is already married," Babette said in her ordinary voice. "Got a kid two years old. Even the Mormons don't have more than one wife at a time, any more."

"Maybe he'll divorce her."

Babette's voice took on a cold sharp edge. "I wouldn't marry him if he was the last man on earth. He's no damn good."

"You can go now," Jake said, appearing behind the service counter and looking taller than he was. "Your check will be in the mail."

Babette turned towards the door, but slowly. "And don't tell me to go to his wife with it. I already did. That's how I found out he has this cute little boy. Poor kid, with him for a father." She walked out into the sunshine, across the parking lot, before Jake could find his tongue. If she was worried, it didn't show.

Jake's face was purple. It was plain that his wife, whatever she was like, hadn't mentioned meeting his girlfriend. Marty could have felt sorry for him if she hadn't been so angry at him on Babette's account. Finally he said in a strangled voice, "You girls better get to work and not just stand there." He took his place behind the register, ready for the mid-afternoon rush. The chrome napkin holders needed filling, but for once he didn't notice.

That might have been the end of it except for scattered gossip, but Jake, the fool, had to pick Marty to talk to. She guessed it was because she was older — he was about twenty-five and kind of an unimportant-looking little guy, the kind who always had to puff himself up. Also by this time she was Good Old Reliable Marty who could do anything around the place, even fix the registers when they got screwed up, and she didn't mind being transferred to the hot kitchen when they were short-handed. He followed her to the door when she started home. Great, she thought, this makes me Teacher's Pet and everyone's going to think I'm on his side. She kept her face blank.

"I want you to keep these broads from talking."

You do, do you? Try it some time, and lots of luck.

"They waste too much time on chitchat the way it is. Half the time the customers don't get any attention."

Not as much time as you wasted fucking the hired help. But that wasn't fair and she knew it. He didn't stand Babette up against the kitchen wall or stretch her out on the order counter, he took her somewhere — motel, probably — and it was reasonable to suppose she went along because she wanted to. They must have had some kind of an understanding before things got this far.

"She's a cheap bitch, and anyhow it's nobody's business but mine."

It was you, then? It would have been smart to deny it, even if no one believed you. You're an idiot, Jake.

"So I know I can count on you."

That's what you think.. She said, "Babette's a friend of mine," although to tell the truth they had never been very chummy. She walked across the parking lot in Babette's very tracks, leaving him standing there.

"Sisterhood is powerful," Thea said when Marty told her. "He'll fire you, but I'm proud of you."

"What else could I do?'

He fired her the next day. Her check was waiting, the ink of the signature not quite dry, when she came in.

Working in a fast food chain has its disadvantages; the smell of hot grease is a minor one. Fired, you don't get two weeks' notice or a severance check, and you're not entitled to unemployment compensation. Nobody stays long enough to build up a base period. She would have sworn that Jake had withheld enough of her pay to cover compensation, or what did all those little figures in the upper right-hand corner of the check mean? Anyway, no comp, as she found when she called the agency from the corner store. And you don't get a reference from an ex-boss who has let you go because you insulted his personal dignity. "Not that he has any, the rat," Thea said. Thea was a very satisfactory friend in a crisis because she knew how to say things Marty could only feel.

"I'm sure going to miss that seventy-some bucks a week."

Was it her imagination, or did Thea brighten up a little? "We still have my welfare check and the ubiquitous rice. We'll get along all right."

She took all their clothes and bedding to the laundromat. She cleaned the house and slapped a coat of whitewash on the bedroom walls. When she couldn't think of anything else to do she went to the welfare office and filed for general assistance, but they didn't give her much encouragement. Unemployment was up, more people were needing help all the time, and the federal government had cut back on all human services. The tourist industry, a big thing in the Sun Belt, was dropping off, and the copper mines were almost surely not going to open. The worker said, "I don't have to tell you, Arizona is poorer than some states."

"More backward, too," Marty said, and walked out. I'm tired of taking shit from people, she told herself. I'd sooner go hungry.

Or live on Thea's check. But then she lived on mine when I had an income and she didn't. That's what sisterhood is. She's right, sisterhood is powerful and you don't have to be a card-carrying feminist to know it. Or am I one and don't know it?

It was a matter of right and wrong. Jake was wrong to knock Babette up when she didn't even know he was married. She was wrong not to go on the Pill, or something. He was wrong, wanting to use Marty for a stooge. Thea was right to be willing to share — Marty had shared with her. Marty admitted it was probably wrong to sass the case worker, but it sure felt good. Besides, how can a black person not know how bad things are? Black people get as much flack as welfare clients, and they couldn't change their skin, like getting a job. If you happen to be black *and* a welfare recipient it must be really bad.

She must have been listening to Thea, all the times she thought she was just turning a polite ear.

"It ain't so bad for black people here," Juan said that evening when they were sitting around in the Ruiz kitchen, drinking sun tea. "Not like Mississippi or Alabama. The Chicanos would be worse off, only most of us have a lot of relatives and everybody chips in when times get bad. Now we're starting to run for office — now our kids are getting to go to college, we've got lawyers and doctors and schoolteachers. I bet I could travel from here to southern Mexico and never have to pay for a hotel room. I got cousins."

Mrs. Ruiz said something in Spanish. Juan laughed. "She says okay, but it goes both ways. We have to do our share too. That's okay, if I have a buck I can find a little something for the widow of my uncle's stepfather. How do you let anybody go hungry?"

"Who's really hard up," Rico put in, "it's the Indians. Specially the Papagos — 'scuse me, the Tohono O'Odhams. They're the low man on the totem pole. Their death rate for kids under one year, it's four times the Anglos. Some of them don't even go to school. See, they're outside the city limits, their reservation, and if they send the kids off to boarding school they can't come home in summer vacation, because of the bus fares. So they get de-Indianized, they forget their own language and their religion and all. So the kid's father keeps him home. But then he can't read or write, and he don't get no job."

"It's bad enough when you talk Spanglish."

"They don't get jobs anyway," Larry said, "because they're Indians."

"Sometimes the Mormons take the kids. Not to adopt them or anything, they let them do housework. They trade their Indian heritage for enough to eat."

Thea carried the tea jar around, filling the glasses. "Makes me feel we're rich."

"You're Anglo," Rico said.

"Come on, you wouldn't trade."

"No, I like what I am. I'm proud of *la raza,* but we've had it tough ever since the Spaniards got here.

That son-of-a-bitch Cortez, they should have pushed him back in the ocean."

"Like my grandfather Shuler, he thought Germans were better than anybody else," Thea said.

They had forgotten about Babette. Rico brought her back into the conversation. "What's she gonna do, your girlfriend?"

"She's going to have the baby."

"Can she stay at home?"

"I guess so. She says her father's been yelling at her, but her mother is all right."

"Because if they won't let her, she could go to the women's shelter for a while. They'll find her a place to live and maybe a job. I think they fix it up with a doctor, too, or a clinic."

"Rico, where do you find out about all these things?"

"All what things?"

"The food giveaway, and the empty houses, and where to go for welfare and how to fill out the forms. It isn't in the paper or on TV, or anything."

Rico lifted his shoulders. "Everybody knows."

"Some is in the buses. In English and Spanish."

Thea's mind was somewhere else. She had figured out the mechanics of survival in the welfare world, mostly by talking to people in the government offices. Now she was brooding over basic principles. "Seems to me as though any woman that wants a baby has a right to have one. Look at all those movie stars and rock singers and people, their pictures are on the covers of magazines, and everyone thinks it's all right."

"Well, but they have money. A lot of people in trouble are poor."

Rico put a hand on his mother's shoulder. "What's poor? You got food on the table, a place to sleep, what else do you need? Want, that's different. The thing is — "Will your friend be a good mother? Will she love the baby?"

"She loves it enough to keep it."

Thea said sternly, "But if she wanted an abortion, that would be up to her."

Juan said, "Sure, but there should be better ways to keep the babies from starting. Not just rubbers, not that pill that makes women sick sometimes. This guy should — did he use something?" He glanced at his mother and stopped, out of respect. No one knew for sure how much English Mama understood. "Didn't he know to do anything, you know?"

"I don't think he cared." Marty had been thinking about that. "He's real young, but he has a kid, and I'd bet he married because his wife was pregnant, only she wasn't his wife yet, of course. I don't think he's very smart."

"Will he give this Babette money, enough to pay the doctor and the hospital?"

"I'm pretty sure he won't. These fast-food places cost a lot, and if you don't make good on it you lose the franchise, and he has a wife and kid, like I said. He probably borrowed to get started. He isn't the kind of guy who ever has much."

"Then you can find out where she lives and tell her about the women's shelter."

"I guess I could."

Larry's eyes met hers. We don't have these problems, they said. See, straight people have their own problems. Once in a while we come out ahead.

She wondered how he knew about her. She had

never said anything, never looked at him when the subject came up, as it was bound to do with two gay guys in the group. And Goddess knew she didn't have anything going. Unless he thought that she and Thea —

A dumb idea. Thea was her sister. Or was she? She would make a nice lover for somebody who didn't judge entirely on looks. She was smart, sweet, and sometimes funny. An intelligent woman, someone who knew there was more to the merchandise than showed in the window, could be happy with Thea. And Thea wouldn't want a lover who only thought about looks, she deserved somebody pretty wonderful.

What am I, a matchmaker? Marty thought. I'm the one who needs a lover. Almost middle-aged, and no love in my life, a few pitiful little memories, that's all. Having fantasies about a truckdriver I'll never see again, and might not like if I knew her.

She stood up. It was time to go home. They hadn't solved all of the world's problems, probably would never even solve their own, but it was good to hash things over and maybe learn a little something once in a while. Made you feel like a person, not an unemployed statistic or a welfare client.

She could get Babette's address from one of the girls at work. I'll just casually drop in and order something, she thought. Jake will be furious, but it's a free country, isn't it?

Chapter 9

"There's something I need to talk to you about."

"Mmmm. Huh?"

It was hot in the bedroom, in spite of the foot-thick adobe walls. The temperature had hit 107 around noon and stayed there. Larry said it was supposed to go down to seventy in the night, but now, at ten, Marty's skin felt hot and the underpants and tee shirt she wore to bed were soaked with sweat. She would have liked to shed them and feel the air on her skin, but Thea slept in pajamas (men's pajamas, thirty cents at Goodwill) and she wasn't going to upset Thea, even if it killed her. At this moment she felt it might.

Thea sat up, wrinkling the already rumpled sheet under them. In the dim moonlight trickling through the window, Marty could see her serious profile. "Won't it wait till morning?" Marty asked.

"It's taken me a long time to get brave enough." Thea's voice quivered a little.

Marty sat up too, hoping the change of position would wake her up. "Okay," she said. "Go ahead. What's biting you?"

"You know Larry and Juan."

"Sure." A dumb remark, whatever it was leading to — and Marty was afraid she knew.

"They live together. I mean, I know Rico and Mama live there too, that's not what I mean. Larry and Juan —"

She was stuck. Marty said helpfully (*oh God, here it comes*), "They love each other, they're lovers, is that what you're talking about?"

"Yes. Well." She was still stuck.

Marty said, exasperated, "Look, I'm not going to stay awake all night talking about Larry and Juan. Whatever they do it's all right with me. What's on your mind?"

"Girls. Women, I mean. You're not supposed to say girls, it down-putting. Women are like that too. I read that book about Beebo Brinker. Women —"

Marty knew you weren't supposed to call women "girls" or "ladies." It was insulting, for some reason. Even that wasn't enough, people spelled it *womyn* or *wimmin* in the magazines Thea had started bringing home — they couldn't afford books, except secondhand ones, but the women's — wimmin's —

87

bookstore had magazines different from any she had ever seen. Thea had told her a story about a little kid in kindergarten who said, "My mother has had a baby woman." She could see where *chick* or *broad* was insulting, why women didn't want to be called *baby,* but what was wrong with *woman,* or even *girl?* The world was so full of real problems, it didn't seem worth making a fuss about.

She was going over all this in her mind because she didn't want to hear what Thea was going to say, but Thea was a gentle bulldozer, she plowed right ahead. "Did you ever do that with women?"

"Sure."

Now she was really in a jam. Thea was going to want to know all about it, what do you do, how do you do it, what does it feel like? And she was supposed to have all the answers. All she knew was what Eileen had done to make her feel so juicy and bubbly and happy. Maybe it wasn't like that for other women. Maybe it was some private quirk of Eileen's. It was humiliating. She couldn't lie to Thea — she had never been much of a liar anyhow — and if she told the truth she was going to be embarrassed to death. There wasn't any in-between. Thea got a lot of information from books, but this time she wanted first-hand data.

For two cents she would get dressed and walk out of there and never go back.

But Thea wasn't asking for information, at least not yet. She said, turning her head away, "Sometimes I've wondered if I was like that. I've never been too interested in men, and I sort of like the idea of being with a woman. Do you have to be a certain way? How do you know about yourself?"

Marty said, "I don't know. Maybe anybody can love anybody else, if they try. Look at the old countries, they used to arrange marriages, and as far as anybody knows they turned out all right. China in the olden days — they didn't even see each other before the wedding. How can you tell?"

"That's different, though. That's normal."

There was no answer to that. How in hell do I know what's normal? Marty wanted to say, but Thea was going on as if she had been thinking about this for a long time and was going to get it over with if it killed her. "What I don't see, what do people *do?* I know how men and women do, they tell you that when you're a little kid in second grade, you watch the mama and papa rabbit mate and after while they have baby rabbits. That's kid stuff. But Larry and Juan — they don't have a place to put anything."

"Sure they do. It's a different place."

"Oh."

"I suppose they hug and kiss too, all the things you do when you like someone." If she could keep Thea on the subject of men it would be all right. That was theoretical; she wasn't supposed to be an expert on what men did or how they felt about it.

It was no use. Weeks of living with Thea had taught her one thing: the kid was quiet, even shy, but when she made up her mind to do something she went ahead and did it. Like going to apply for welfare even though she was scared to death of the case workers and didn't understand the forms. She plodded on, looking away as if Marty could read her expression in the dark. "But women —"

Marty said, "Come off it. You've been reading all those books — they don't leave much out, I guess."

She shut her eyes, wishing this was tomorrow and this idiotic conversation all in the past.

"Sure, I know in a general way. It's only — it seems kind of unlikely. What they do and how they do it, like something somebody made up." Thea's voice quavered.

Marty had to smile. Thea's mind worked in such a logical way. Men didn't have a place to put anything, women didn't have anything to put. As simple as that. "They have hands and mouths. Isn't that enough?"

"Oh." Marty could hear the wheels go around.

"Didn't anyone ever tell you the facts of life?"

"Only when it was one of each, like pieces of machinery fitting together."

"Don't sound like much fun."

"What I always wanted," Thea said in a voice so low that Marty had to lean closer to hear, "was someone who cared about me, someone I could care about. Like going to sleep snuggled up against somebody and knowing we belonged together. I guess that's silly."

"Make sense to me." Marty sighed. She might not have much experience, she might not know much, but she probably knew more than Thea. "That's the way it starts. Then you keep wanting more. See, one thing sort of leads to another. What you finally get is the most there is, if you're lucky."

Thea seemed to be thinking it over. "I don't suppose you'd want to try it. With me? Like just being close, for starters. Of course I'm not good-looking, I never expected to be close to anybody. Men always want good-looking girls — women. I suppose it's the same with women?"

It sounded possible, like something you could do for a friend. Goddess knew, she, Marty, had lain awake enough nights wishing she had someone, anyone. She moved a little so she could pull Thea's pajama top over her head, then bent to unfasten her pants. Thea froze, but Marty pulled them off anyway. She stripped off her pants and tee shirt, noticing that her hands were shaking. "You want me to light the lamp?"

"No, it's too embarrassing. I'm so ugly."

Marty didn't think so, but she knew what she meant. Thea had probably been ashamed to undress in front of the girls in her gym class, when she was a kid — when you have something wrong with you, you keep it hidden, like putting Covermark on a birthmark. Besides, she and Thea had been living together like sisters, and now all of a sudden they were on the edge of something personal and scary. It was like standing on the edge of the Grand Canyon, terrified of falling over and wondering what it would feel like if you jumped.

She put a hand on Thea's shoulder, a thin shoulder with the bones sticking out. Thea sat still. She, Marty, was supposed to know what to do. It wasn't fair.

She moved the hand down, over little ribs she could have counted if she'd been in the right frame of mind for number games. Small hips, but more rounded than she would have thought from seeing Thea in shorts. Pubic hair wet with sweat — it was a hot night, all right. She moved upward, found Thea's adolescent breast and took it carefully in her hand. It was the breast of a little girl just ready to grow up, waiting for her first period. She leaned over and took the nipple carefully in her mouth. Thea stiffened, but was silent.

She moved down again. Now she wasn't thinking only of Thea, she was starting to feel the sweet urgency she had felt in the hospital, when Eileen touched her. She had to go on. She didn't want to think about the hospital, even though it was tied up with her memory of Eileen.

Gently, she pushed apart the little soft lips that held the secret part of Thea, and pushed a careful finger in. Thea moved. It was hardly more than a shiver, but it encouraged her to go on. She knew more than she thought. Was she remembering this, or was it something that came to her naturally, like a baby born knowing how to suck? Nobody ever tells you anything you really want to know.

She moved her finger, pushing it in deeper, feeling all the little folds and bumps, memorizing them with a fingertip. The inside of Thea didn't feel like her own self when she explored her own hot and hungry body. Was there as much difference here as in faces? Would every woman be a new experience, different from the rest?

Thea moved a little, then a little more. A wetness spread over Marty's probing hand.

Now she had to go on, not for Thea's sake but for her own. Had to, even if she died for it. She found a movement that felt right, and circled, pressed, stroked and teased. Found at the entrance, backing away from the wet depth she had just discovered, the hard little stub standing up and waiting for her. Found that she wanted to suck it, and moved convulsively to spread herself across Thea's welcoming body with her tongue flicking back and forth over the little button under no orders from her. Smart tongue, it knew what to do without being told.

She didn't know how long it went on, minutes or hours or forever. She was in a strange place, a place she had never been before. She didn't know when Thea moved and moaned and heaved upward and then lay back, panting. She didn't know when the finger left Thea's wetness and found her own special place and moved frantically until the widening circles of feeling broke, shattered, washed her up on some shore where she lay and felt the waves ebbing away. And here she was on their mattress, with Thea clutched to her, sobbing in pleasure, and then she came back to time and place in a hurry. "Did I hurt you?"

"No, I feel wonderful." Thea tightened her arms around Marty and lay as close as she could get. Everything seemed to fit together, even though they were not the same shape or size. Thea's head fitted into Marty's shoulder. Marty's fingers curved over Thea's little-girl breast.

She had to tell the truth. You couldn't lie to someone with whom you had been tossed ashore on that strange tide. "I'm not all that experienced."

"You're wonderful."

"Maybe we'll get better at it."

"Are we going to do it again?"

It hadn't occurred to Marty to look ahead. "Only if we want to." But how could she stop here, after discovering this thing?

"I want you to do it again. I want to do it for you, if I can learn how. It's the most wonderful thing — I never dreamed —"

"Practice makes perfect." Marty was suddenly

calm and full of self-esteem. She was also hungry, and suddenly thirsty.

She didn't know if what had happened to Thea was an orgasm. She had always supposed orgasm were something you had to learn — after doing it long enough you got some kind of a total reaction. But something had happened, and Thea was happy with it. As for what had happened to her, there wasn't any question. It was like floating up through the roof and coming down in some new country where everything was strange and wonderful; where you didn't only see with your eyes and hear with your ears but experienced everything, magnified and multiplied, with your whole body. She could hardly wait to do it again. Except, of course, that now she was getting sleepy as well as thirsty.

She fell asleep, clutching Thea, before she could mobilize herself into getting up and getting a drink.

They awoke when the sun came up at six, hot and sweaty and astonished to find themselves naked. Thea leaned over to kiss Marty, shyly. "Do you mind that I'm so ugly?"

"You're beautiful," Marty said, meaning it. This skinny little body was precious to her; it filled her with a wish to shelter and cherish it. She hugged Thea carefully, as if she might break. This small thin body, with one arm a little longer than the other and one leg a little smaller, with all of its hair the same yellowish color, with the narrow face anxious and full of smiles at the same time — it was Thea. "You're not ugly, you're beautiful."

As if Thea knew better, she smiled. "You need your eyes examined."

They pulled themselves upright. "We sure need

baths," Marty said. That meant heating water on the hot plate or in the percolator and pouring it into the bathroom basin, diluting the cold water, which came in lukewarm all summer long anyway. It meant washing yourself in sections and never quite getting all the soap off. They both longed for a real bathtub, or failing that, a washtub like the one Larry and Juan used. You could stand up in a washtub and pour water over yourself. You could scrooch down in it and get your lower half wet. If they ever found a tub for sale cheap, they would buy it and carry it home on the bus. Plenty of people in this neighborhood still washed things out in galvanized tubs, old Mexican ladies, but nobody ever sold one or gave it away, they were used until the holes couldn't be soldered any more.

Thea said, "Let's have coffee first. I feel sort of dehydrated."

They ambled into the kitchen, not touching, embarrassed by their nakedness and enjoying it at the same time. Thea ran water into the coffee pot and plugged it into the dangling socket. "They got it all wrong in the Bible."

"How do you mean?"

"Adam and Eve were ashamed of their bodies after they ate the fruit. I was ashamed of mine before. They got it backward."

"Well, it was men that wrote the Bible. Men don't know anything about women."

That seemed to settle it.

Chapter 10

Now that neither of them was working, they could do things together. They swept the bumpy floors — sand collected on the lower side of each sloping room — and washed dishes, took their skimpy baths together, and bought tortillas and green chilis at the mama-papa store. They sauntered home in the increasing morning heat talking about Mexican food — after all they were eating, they had about two hundred dollars saved, and Thea's welfare review was favorable. They were all right.

Marty went along to the branch library and took

out a murder mystery on Thea's card. Thea was reading a book by Mary Daly which she, Marty, didn't understand, but she was proud of Thea's growing interest in women's history. More and more, Thea was hanging out at the women's bookstore, even though she had no money for books. She came home with a button or a flimsy-paper magazine, and stories of talk that went on; she was meeting this one and that one, and learning. "It's better than a class at the U."

There wasn't room for both of them in Rico's car on food-box day, so Marty, as the muscular one, rode along with Juan and Larry, and Thea took their clothes to the laundromat. Mama Ruiz was cooking lunch for all of them. "First thing you learn on welfare," Rico quoted his mother, "you don't need meat if you have rice and beans." He grinned. "I got an Anglo stomach. I'd like a hamburger."

Thea kept wondering if there was some way she could learn Spanish without paying for it. Of course she knew a lot of words, and she and Mama filled in with gestures and smiles, but she wanted the whole thing — grammar, tenses, verb endings. You learned from the notices posted in public buildings and the ads in the buses. She looked for secondhand textbooks as she went through the resale shops.

The food-box run had become routine. You had to have a person from each household, the food varied from month to month — always rice and pinto beans, though — and there were different volunteers, all pleasant and polite. Today Marty shoved her boxes into the back of the car, pleased to notice that they were getting canned tomatoes and string beans, evaporated milk instead of powdered, a box apiece of oatmeal, and some noodles. Then she saw that Larry had set his carton on the ground and was bent over, coughing. She waited. Larry straightened up, gasping and choking, and wiped his face on a sleeve. She asked, "What's the matter?"

"This damn summer cold. They never seem to go away."

She looked him over. He was thin, but then he always was; he was one of those rangy boys with a skinny neck and lantern jaw. A New England type, Thea said. You couldn't call him handsome, but he looked *nice.* He and the Ruiz boys were like part of her family; she hardly ever really looked at them. She said casually, "You've lost a little weight, seems to me. You shouldn't skip your meals just because it's hot."

There was no use saying, "Go to a doctor, have a checkup." Who had a doctor? A hospital emergency room would cost at least eighty dollars — enough to feed a family for a month. Poor people learned to get along without doctors and medicine. She said, "Maybe Vitamin C. That's supposed to be good for colds."

It was a very hot day, the sky clouded in promise — or threat — of rain that never came, the monsoon season overdue with its high winds and sheets of blowing sand. Nervous weather. Cicadas sang in the vacant lots and kids skate-boarded along the sidewalks, dodging shopping mamas and church-going nanas; every day there was a sprinkle of old ladies at Saint Augustine's. In more affluent neighborhoods the snowbirds had all gone home and the year-round residents played in their swimming pools and broiled big steaks on outdoor grills. Here in the barrio life went on pretty much as usual, except that more folks sat in their backyards and visited after supper. There was a small-town feeling in the air, although Tucson had hit the half-million mark and thought of itself as a metropolis. They were building a huge ugly skyscraper downtown; Marty was pleased when the palm trees they planted around it withered and died. Some architect from up north had romantic ideas about southwestern buildings. She liked the small-town feeling and hoped it wouldn't change.

She felt great. Partly it was the heat; partly it was not having to go to work mostly, though, it was Thea and the feeling that was growing between them. Without expecting it, without talking about it, they had started taking for granted that what they had was more than sexual excitement. She knew Thea had never made love with anyone before, had taken for granted that she never would, but she seemed to take to it naturally and, now that the ice was broken, was turning out to be more inventive in bed than Marty. It was great.

The second night of their relationship, when Marty had been ravenous to go to bed and scared at the same time — suppose Thea had changed her mind? Thea had stepped up behind her and put asking arms around her, closing hands over Marty's breasts. "Let's go to bed. I want to do something nice for you this time." And she had, starting with the careful gentle motions Marty had used on her but getting more and more urgent until they were both carried away and they finally fell asleep even though neither of them wanted to stop. Thea was a ear-nibbler, a finger-sucker, a toe-sucker. She made tickles on Marty's behind and ripples of feeling down Marty's thighs, and she went to sleep with her fingers inside Marty and little waves of feeling still ebbing away. Love was such an abundant thing, they could have it every day for a lifetime and there would still be a lot left, so why be greedy?

Marty couldn't help it, she felt greedy.

The third time they tried making love to each other at the same time, and to their surprise, it worked. Marty, with her head at the foot of the bed, with Thea's clutching legs against her cheeks, had a hard time keeping her mind on what was happening up there on the pillow, when everything inside her seemed to be turning to liquid and pouring out under Thea's seeking tongue. It was almost too much.

The next day Thea went to the library, her source for all information, and got out a fat book called *Studies in the Psychology of Sex*, by someone named Ellis. This old man (the picture of him in the front of the book had a long gray beard) seemed to have lived a long time ago, but people told him the most astonishing things. They had to tear themselves away from it to fix their meals, and Marty filed away some of the case histories in her mind to try some day, when she got brave enough.

Larry laughed when he saw the book. Sure, they taught it in colleges. "If you want to see something really exciting, you ought to go to the porn shops. I warn you though, their prices are out of sight." He took her to one, and she looked around while the young man behind the counter tactfully paid no attention. The magazines were all wrapped in plastic, so you couldn't see what you were getting until you bought it, but there were strange things in the glass case: big pink candles shaped like male organs (did they turn on gay guys, and why?) and vibrators with nubby attachments, and things whose use she couldn't guess. But why would you want that stuff when you could have a living palpitating responding human body to play with?

Larry put a quarter in a little machine and she got about a minute of what she supposed was meant to be a dirty film, though it was so badly lighted and moved so fast it was hard to tell what the people were supposed to be doing. "It's kind of grubby," she told Larry when they came out into the glare and the traffic. "I'd like to see a slow movie of women making love out in the woods, or somewhere."

"I know what you mean, but it's all some people have. Old guys who are afraid to cruise, they go in there and watch that stuff and it's better than nothing. That's the only excitement they ever get."

Why should getting old make any difference? she wondered. Couldn't an old guy find another old guy and share his life? Or did they only want casual pickups, no involvement? She couldn't believe it. Men and women were different, but not that different.

Thea came running out when the car stopped. She lifted a carton from the back and started in with it. Larry grabbed it away from her, took a few steps, then set it down as another spasm of coughing overtook him. Marty said, "You better get some cough drops or something."

"Mama made me some onion soup."

The old car chugged away. Marty was glad Mama and Rico were waiting on the sidewalk; Larry shouldn't be lifting things if it made him cough. A flicker of worry crossed her mind and vanished. Everybody has colds, and in Arizona the seasons are scrambled.

Inside the kitchen, Thea kissed her. "*La mesa,*" she said, pointing to the table. "*Comida.*" She folded her hands under her cheek and shut her eyes. "*Duremo. Cama. Amor.*"

"You're a fast learner." They dissolved into idiotic laughter. Marty said sternly, "Let's get this stuff put away."

"Did they try to convert you?"

"No, I don't think that lady does it any more. There was a nice old one. She said, you know, we are welcome to go to church any time. I don't mind that, if they don't push."

"It might be kind of nice to go to church once in a while, but I'm not going to be converted."

Marty was lining up cans on the shelf. "Even the Sallies can't make you be converted. You have to listen, but you don't have to believe it."

"I heard that the Sallies report illegal refugees. It might not be true, but the Sanctuary people won't send them there. That's a drag," Thea said angrily. "This is supposed to be a free country. People are supposed to come here when they're oppressed. That was the idea in the first place, wasn't it? Hell, now you don't get a fair shake even if you were born and raised here."

"Nobody's going to drag you out of bed in the middle of the night and shoot you," Marty said reasonably.

"Some woman came by while you were gone. They're having a picnic in the park Sunday, for Central America. You want to go?"

"I don't know." She suspected that Thea did want to go, planned to go, and was only asking to be polite. "It seems kind of public."

"They have rallies on campus all the time."

It might be nice to go somewhere, Marty thought. How long was it since she had gone anywhere just for fun? They couldn't afford movies, and going anyplace meant bus fare. You went to work if you had a job, to the food-box church if you knew someone who had a car, Thea went to the library, that was her idea of a good time. Marty changed the subject. "What are we going to do between now and then?"

"Take naps," Thea said promptly. Something that was almost a dimple popped out on her left cheek. "We'll think of something."

"What do you call sheets and pillowcases in Spanish?"

Thea didn't know, but it would be easy to find out. "You know why poor people have so many kids? They can't afford to go to the movies. That's one thing we don't have to worry about."

Marty privately thought she wouldn't mind going to an air-conditioned movie. On the other hand, she wouldn't mind lying down on *la cama* with Thea and seeing what developed. She cupped a hand over Thea's small responsive breast as they walked into the bedroom. "Sometimes you're fairly smart," she said, as if it didn't really matter and all they had to do was find some way to pass the time until it cooled off.

Chapter 11

Marty had always known that things were uneven. Her mom when sober had talked in quotes — probably still did; it was about twelve years since Marty had seen her or heard from her. Never rains but it pours. Chicken one day and feathers the next. Them that has, gets.

The only time Marty ever had a job she really liked, someone came along and offered her another.

She supposed it might be the same way with love. She was hungry all those years, not brave enough to go out and look for someone. Now she had Thea —

sweet and warm and inventive — well, either she was inventive or she had found the kind of book she was looking for and was reading it behind Marty's back, which was unlikely. Thea was a sharer. "Hey, listen to this!" Marty not only liked what they did in bed, at mealtime she found herself looking at Thea across the card table, which so far was the only table they had, with a feeling of tenderness and amusement. Without planning ahead, she figured she could probably live with Thea for the rest of her life and not complain. So what happened?

She was walking down the street minding her own business, or to be more exact, getting ready to mind Babette's business. Now that the first excitement of having a lover had died down some, she had finally remembered Babette and her promise to check up on the girl; she didn't know if it was curiosity or concern or some of both, but she had told Larry she would tell Babette about the women's shelter, if she needed to know. That was little enough to do for a sister in trouble. The concern hit about the same time she had a free day. The house was clean, Thea had gone to the university to file one more application for a grant — waste of time, Marty thought. But she was glad Thea could keep on hoping, and proud of her determination. It was a fine day for August, a brisk breeze off the desert; she had a low-income bus card which let her go places for a quarter. It all fitted together. She put on clean jeans and her favorite tee shirt and started out for Burger Palace with a feeling of adventure. It was a long time since she had gone anywhere.

She walked along feeling good, enjoying the busy neighborhood, the traffic whizzing by — so different from their street — and the prospect of seeing the girls at the Palace. She didn't look for a moment when a big transcontinental truck pulled up alongside. Then a tall good-looking woman at the wheel rolled down the window, never mind the air-conditioning, and a low-pitched voice asked lazily, "Can I take you somewhere?"

She was too surprised to answer.

"I do know you. Your name's Marty. Work at Burger Palace."

"I did. I got fired."

"Well, get in. I'll take you wherever you're going."

"I'm going to Burger Palace." She was in the truck, she was sitting alongside this gorgeous woman without knowing how she got there.

"Going to ask for your job back?"

"No way. It wouldn't do any good." She surprised herself by laughing. "It isn't really funny. This girl I worked with, she got pregnant —" She supposed it wasn't an unusual story, girls got knocked up all the time, but she didn't know those other women, that made a difference.

"I'll go with you." The truck started smoothly and quietly, not like Rico's heap. "You're Martha. Martha what?"

"Brown." She wished she had a more romantic name, something foreign, or like a movie star. "Everybody calls me Marty." Everybody who? Thea and Larry and the Ruizes. She didn't know anyone else.

"I'm Joan Schiller. Let's go see if anyone knows anything about your Babette."

There were three new people behind the registers,

all teenaged and pretty, all looking alike in their little orange caps and aprons. One was black and one was kind of plump, nevertheless, they all looked alike somehow. The wives from the air force base with their little blond kids whining in the supermarket, the working girls she saw on the bus — home permanents, eye liner, bored expressions — they looked alike, too. But the tall cool woman walking beside her didn't look like anyone else, she could have been an actress or a business executive. On a scale from one to ten Marty would have rated her a ten for looks and poise.

Helen looked out from the kitchen. "Hi, Marty! How's everything?"

"Fine. I just dropped in to see how everybody was." She couldn't say, I'm living on my roommate's welfare check.

Jake came out of the back room. When he saw her his mouth dropped open. She had often heard about that but had never seen it, she always supposed it was something people who wrote books made up. Jake said in a mean voice that sounded a little quavery, "If you're looking for work, there's nothing here."

"Who said anything about work? I came in for a Jumbo and a cup of coffee." She looked at Joan. "What's yours?"

"Same, with fries. But see here, I'll —"

This was going to break her — Thea's money, too — but she was going to pay for both of them. There are times when you have to do something you can't afford. She laid the emergency five on the counter and let Joan pick up the tray. In a corner booth, she smiled at a couple of regulars — Mrs. Scheff having her ten o'clock coffee, old Mr. Turnbull who must have outlasted a dozen cashiers. It was odd how you figured that things must have changed for everybody else just because they did for you, and here was the rest of the world going on its regular way.

Helen came back to their booth with no excuse at all, Jake glowering at her. If there had been a line of people waiting he would have said something, but it was a slow spell, four or five customers taking their time with coffee or iced tea, in no hurry to go out into the heat and glare. Marty remembered what she was there for. "Helen, do you ever see Babette?"

"Oh sure. Her folks go to the same church as mine. They're gong to adopt the baby." Helen smiled. "She's got a new boyfriend, would you believe it? Sticking out the way she's starting to and all, she's gone into maternity dresses and she looks huge. She was in here with him. 'We're going to be married after the baby comes,' she says, as cool as can be, and he nods. I thought Jake was going to have a stroke."

Marty considered the pleasant idea of Jake having a stroke. She could see that Joan was enjoying it too. "Well, good for her. I hope everything works out all right." There didn't seem to be any point in mentioning the women's shelter; Babette had worked everything out for herself.

She ate her burger without really tasting it. Weeks of putting them together hadn't dulled her taste for the good grilled meat, the lettuce and tomato a sharp shock of onion, but the consciousness of Joan on the other side of the table wiped everything else out of her mind. As for Joan, she sat eating her sandwich and sipping coffee without, as far as Marty could tell, anything at all on her mind. She had one of those oval faces, and she looked calm. Marty couldn't help wondering what went on behind that tanned face, behind those big brown eyes. It would be exciting to find out, to move her to passion or laughter or even surprise.

Back in the truck, the air conditioner purring, Joan said, "I'm ahead of schedule. Would you like to go somewhere? Reid Park, and feed the ducks?"

"Sure." She didn't know anything about Reid Park, she had never been there, and she wasn't interested in ducks, but if that was what Joan liked to do it was all right with her. As for schedules she didn't have one, except to be home by supper time, hours from now.

Reid Park wasn't cool, no place was, but it was shady. There were real trees, not just palo verde and a random mulberry or two. Birds sang in the branches. People sat under the ramadas, eating and cooling off, and kids ran around yelling. There was a lagoon. And there were ducks, brown ones and white and some with iridescent blue-green heads and necks, paddling around in the murky water or waddling along the shore. Joan had stopped to pick up a loaf of bread, and she broke it in two and handed half to Marty. The ducks waited, beady-eyed and watchful. This was old stuff to them; this was what human beings were for.

Marty tore off bits of bread and tossed them, but her mind wasn't on ducks or on the small birds that swooped down from tree branches and picked up the bread. Joan said, "I like for the little fellows to get some," but the sparrows and doves looked well fed. Joan opened two cans of Pepsi and handed one to

Marty. The sweet stuff tasted good, though she knew the phony sugar would only make her thirsty again. Thea said that was what it was for, to keep people drinking, to keep making money for the company. Give her sun tea or plain water, Thea said. She didn't want to think about Thea.

They sat down on two uncomfortable rocks at the water's edge and Joan sighed. "Sure peaceful out here. Now tell me about yourself. What do you do?"

"Not much of anything. I'm like a lot of people, I don't have a job. Only some of them don't have a place to sleep, and I do."

"You live with someone?"

Marty wasn't sure which way this was meant. Did she share a house with someone, or did she have a relationship? Also she didn't want to think about Thea, much less talk about her. She tried to think of a good lie, but nothing came. "Yes. We're living on my roommate's welfare, but I'm trying to find something."

"What's she like?"

"Small and blonde." She wasn't going into any details, she wasn't going to say that they had only been lovers for a couple of weeks, or mention that Thea had had polio. She looked at a white duck that kept bobbing into the water head-down, its tail sticking up.

"Are you monogamous?"

Marty stared. "I suppose so. We haven't been together very long." That sounded as if she might not be monogamous once the novelty wore off, an impression she wasn't sorry to give, but she felt that anything she might add would only make it worse. (Larry said, "Don't give 'em anything but your name,

110

rank and serial number, and never volunteer." That was army, but he said it worked for johns, too. Larry knew a lot about johns.)

Joan looked thoughtful. "Georgina and I tried being monogamous. It worked for about a year. Then we started looking around and she got hot pants for a woman in her office. She told me about it. We've always been honest with each other, that's why we've lasted so long. No point in breaking up a good relationship because of a temporary itch. We've been primary lovers for almost eight years, we'll probably be together forever, but we're both free to go off and play with somebody else. It works all right."

Marty knew guys were like that. They moved in together and had joint bank accounts and all, but they made out with other people when they felt like it. But women? It sounded reasonable, it sounded liberated, but she couldn't help wondering, "Don't you ever get jealous?"

"What for? Sex isn't something that you run out of, you don't just get so much and have to hoard it. The more you do it the better it gets."

Come to think of it, Eileen probably had a steady lover when she was meeting her in the linen room. Marty had never thought about that before. Did she tell her lover she was fooling around with a patient? She would never know.

"We've internalized male values so long, we've come to believe in all kinds of idiotic things. Virginity — thank goodness that's on the way out — and monogamy and possessiveness. There's nothing noble about being jealous, that's kid stuff. You can't own people."

"Well, no." That sounded reasonable. It sounded

111

like some of the ideas Thea was always bringing home.

"Your body belongs to you." Joan stood up. "Come on, I'll take you home."

"You don't need to do that. Just drop me at a bus stop."

"No, but I will."

Marty sat silently in the cool from the air conditioner. She didn't want Joan to see where she lived, the broken sidewalks, the dark-skinned children playing in the streets, the houses that had been there since Territorial times all looked poor. But Joan, stopping in front of the house, was delighted. "It's wonderful. It's like a street in Spain or the south of France, the whitewashed walls and all. Are there gardens in back?"

"Little yards with fences between. I guess anybody would make a garden." She had never thought about it before.

"Maybe I'll come and see you some day."

"Sure. Thea too."

Joan made a dismissing gesture, Marty hadn't meant to speak of Thea. It had just slipped out. She said hastily, "We don't have a bathtub, and no heat but a fireplace."

"I suppose there are places in Provence and Andalusia where they don't have bathtubs."

Marty didn't know where Provence and Andalusia were, but they sounded romantic and interesting. "Thanks for the ride. And the ducks."

"Thanks for the Jumbo and Coke. I guess you don't have a telephone — what's the address? Or no, wait." She tore a deposit slip out of her checkbook, a posh checkbook imprinted with her name in gold block letters. "You call me when you have some free time." She leaned to kiss Marty. The kiss landed on her mouth, not on the cheek she automatically turned, and it stung like a bee. It lasted, too. Marty was kissing back, with no conscious intention of doing any such thing, with no thought for the neighbors, without even wondering if Thea was home and watching from the window.

Joan pushed her away and opened the truck door, laughing. "Give me a call, Marty. I'd like to know you better."

Marty went in, not sure whether she wanted to see Joan again or whether she was terrified by the idea. Anyway, Joan had given her enough to think about for a while.

Thea was still out. Marty slipped off her zori and sat down at the kitchen table to think things over.

Thea came home looking wilted but triumphant. She had applied for a grant in Humanities, whatever that meant, and had filed applications for three jobs. One was for library assistant, which she explained didn't call for any special skill but only meant she would be replacing books on shelves and mending torn pages with scotch tape. Marty could see that the idea of spending seven and a half hours a day in a library exactly fitted Thea's notion of a perfect job. With all her heart she hoped it would come through.

She was feeling a little guilty. There was no reason why she shouldn't tell Thea about Joan, this woman she had met twice. "I just happened to meet this woman, this truck driver who came into the Burger Palace when I was working there, and we went out to Reid Park and fed the ducks." It would make an interesting story, but she had a feeling that

113

now was not the time. She did describe Jake's reaction and Babette's good news — at least, Helen seemed to think it was good news; she herself wouldn't have wanted to have a baby and give it up, much less marry anyone. But Babette was getting what she wanted, and the baby would grow up thinking she was its sister; at least she would know the kid was all right. That was more than most unwed mothers had.

Fall in the pot and come up smelling like roses, her mom would have said.

They were still sitting at the table, drinking sun tea and trying to cool off, when there was a tap on the door and at once, without waiting for an answer, Rico came in. "Can you come to our house right away? Larry is sick, awful sick. He can't breathe."

Thea said, "Oh God," and pulled on her sandals and followed him out of the door, leaving Marty to trail along.

The Ruiz house was in an uproar. Mama stood beside the bed with a glass of water in her hand. Larry was stretched out purple-faced and gasping for breath, Juan holding him by the shoulders, a couple of unidentified neighbors sympathetic and helpless, in the doorway. Marty bent down and touched Larry's cheek. "He's burning hot. His cold is worse, isn't it?"

Mama Ruiz said something. Juan translated, "She says this is more than a cold. She says he should be in a hospital, but how can that be when he doesn't have any money? Hospitals are for rich people." Juan looked angry. "Even County Hospital, it started for poor people and now it costs a fortune to go there, like the rest."

114

Thea took charge. "Where's the nearest telephone?"

"At Hernandes', if they paid the bill yet. Or at the store, but that costs a quarter."

Thea looked at Rico, who took off, looking glad to get out of there.

"I knew he had a cold," Marty said. "It's hung on for a long time." She tried to remember how long, but who notices a cold? You sneeze, you cough, you run a little fever, your joints ache for a day or two, then you start getting well. Nobody pays any attention. Now that she thought of it, Larry seemed to have been sick for a long time, always tired, but who didn't get tired in hot weather?

He had lost weight. His cheekbones stuck out. She said, "We'll get him to a hospital. They can give him antibiotics or something."

Thea and Juan took out after Rico. She could sound Anglo, she could sound authoritative — Marty could hear her: get an ambulance over here and be quick about it. Rico was too polite. Thea could be high-handed if she had to.

It was half an hour before the ambulance got there. It seemed forever. By that time there were more people in the room — bad news travels fast — and the young paramedics shooed them out of the way. They rolled Larry onto a stretcher and strapped him down. He roused up. One of them gave him a shot in the arm. Juan said, "I'm going along." No one paid any attention. One of the uniformed men wrapped a blood-pressure cuff around Larry's arm and the other laid a digital thermometer on his forehead. Just like on TV, Marty thought, she had seen it a hundred times, but this wasn't a soap opera, Larry was their friend, and in real life the good guys didn't always win. This was the guy who shared his rice and beans with her and Thea when their food ran low.

They would put him in an oxygen tent, and strap his arm to a jar of something, and when he got better they would all go to see him and he would give them hell for being so worried. All they really had to worry about was the hospital bill, which none of them could pay, so why worry? He would be listed as indigent, or maybe they would put him on AHCCS, which the well-insured members of the state legislature thought was taking care of poor people. If you were sick enough someone had to take care of you even if you couldn't pay, if you made enough fuss.

Juan started to follow the paramedics and the stretcher. They shooed him back. Thea said clearly, "He is the brother, he's the next of kin," and they looked unsure; Juan was certainly Hispanic and Larry looked like a New England farmer, which was what he had been until he hit out for the bright lights. Still, you never knew. Juan climbed into the ambulance and crouched down beside the stretcher. Nobody was going to keep him from going along with Larry, no matter where they were taking him; he wasn't going to argue about it, he was just going along. Marty hoped he would get a gay doctor, or someone who knew the score.

None of them got much sleep that night. Juan stopped by on his way from the hospital, about eleven, to report that they had taken Larry in when they saw what a high fever he was running. He was out of his head by that time, he didn't know where he was. Juan had filled out form after form after form, making up whatever he didn't know; the names of Larry's parents and the childhood diseases he had had, and many other things they didn't need to know. He would never be able to remember what he had put down on all those papers. "It doesn't matter," Thea told him. "Nobody ever looks at those forms. They're just a way to keep the family busy."

What mattered was that Larry was in a nice clean hospital bed, with nurses looking after him; he had a needle in his arm (Juan turned pale) and tubes up his nose. If they only wouldn't send him home when they found he had no money, that was what Mama was worrying about. "They will keep him until the fever goes away," Juan assured her, although he wasn't sure even of that. "When you're in, you're in. We can take care of him when he gets better."

"But what do they think it is?"

"Probably pneumonia. His lungs are full and he has trouble breathing." They knew, they had heard him trying to breathe. "They will run more tests. I'll find out tomorrow."

"Will they let us see him?"

"Only me. I'm the next of kin." They had to laugh, worried and tired as they were. There was Juan, brown as his Indian grandfather — "Don't call me Spanish, I'm proud of *la raza*" — and there was angular Larry whose whiskers came in straw-colored. Someone had been humane enough to believe him, or pretend to. Juan said he had to go home, because Mama would be waiting for him. Thea said, "You go to bed. You need some sleep."

Marty didn't feel like sleeping. Or making love.

117

They lay side by side on the wrinkling sheet and were silent. After a while Thea's hand came to rest on Marty's shoulder. I'm here, the hand said, and I care about you. Finally they slept, more or less.

Juan went to the hospital in the morning, stopping to borrow Marty's bus card because he couldn't pay full fare. She said she wasn't going anywhere. "Keep it as long as you need it." They watched him walk off, scared of the medical establishment but determined; nothing was going to keep him away from Larry. He would find out what was the matter with Larry, what was being done for him and, maybe, when he could come home. If Larry woke up he was going to be there. For himself he could never had been so brave, but for Larry he would push his way into the head doctor's office if he had to.

Neither of them felt much like talking. Marty washed all their dishes — there weren't many — and scrubbed the shelf and put them all back. Thea went out with a pair of scissors and cut the tallest weeds in the yard. They had a thin slice of sandy soil defined by a sagging fence on each side, not in good enough repair to keep children or chickens in but meant to mark off their rental property from the neighbors'. Thea sat on the back step and considered planting some flowers. What would grow in this climate, without having to be watered? None of the neighbors had gardens, except for a few petunias and geraniums planted in tubs or jars. Maybe Mama Ruiz would give her a geranium slip and she could carry water to it after sundown, from the bathroom tap. It would be nice to have something growing in their yard.

118

She wasn't going to think about Larry.

Juan came in at eleven to say that Larry had pneumonia and they were going to run some more tests. At least they were letting him stay in the hospital. He drank a glass of sun tea and went home to tell the family.

Thea said jumpily, "There's something funny about this. Pneumonia isn't that hard to diagnose."

"Maybe they try out new drugs on patients who can't pay, or something." Her experience with the welfare establishment had left Marty skeptical about its motives. If you got something for nothing, watch out. Except for the food boxes, of course, but even there they hoped you would be converted.

Food boxes were several days in the past and Thea's welfare check was a week in the future. They had pinto beans for lunch, cooked slowly with a lot of garlic. When it was over Thea said, "I don't feel like staying home. Let's walk down to Fourth."

"It's hotter than hell out there."

"I don't care. I'm still looking for a washtub, or even an old bathtub would be all right, only where would we put it?"

"Do we have any money?" It was the first time Marty had thought about yesterday's extravagance. She ought to own up to it, but how could she without going into the whole story, Reid Park, ducks, goodbye kiss and all? Her silence bothered Thea, who promised, "I won't buy anything if it costs more than a dollar."

Fourth Avenue, Tucson's version of Greenwich Village, was almost deserted today. A few well-dressed people came out of one of the fancy restaurants; the others poked in and out of the retail shops. They

119

were always planning to count the resale shops —
Thea's guess was fifteen in five blocks, counting both
sides of the street and not counting the ones that
specialized in things like hand-crafted furniture and
vintage clothing. If you had a Chanel dress or a
World War Two outfit with padded shoulders, this
was the place to dispose of it. The clothes Marty and
Thea bought in Value Valley, Goodwill and the
Salvation Army store had never been high style and
consequently they would be presentable as long as the
threads hung together.

Even Value Valley looked sleepy. The customers
who had been there in the early morning, trailing
small children, were home now making lunch for
those children or putting them down for naps. The
teenagers were somewhere else; probably ordering
Jumbos at Burger Palace, Marty thought. She made
her way purposefully through the quiet aisles looking
for used sneakers and, of course the washtub they
kept on needing.

No washtubs today. No big china bowls either —
these counted as antiques and sold for more than
most people could afford. One of the girls at Burger
Palace had a funny story about being asked out for
dinner and finding a china chamber pot, lavishly hand
painted, on the middle of the lace-covered table,
holding flowers. It was odd what things were antiques
these days: old fruit jars, copper wash boilers,
stereoscopes and views, old postcards and
photographs. Thea liked to look at such things but
never expected to own any of them. Thrift shops, on
the other hand, offered things people needed at prices
they could pay.

They found a good fifteen-cent egg beater and a pair of red socks for a dime, and Thea spent some time in front of the bookshelves. "They're mostly *Readers Digest* condensed junk," she reported. "Let's go to Dairy Queen and have a cone."

"Can we afford it?" But Marty tagged along and took a couple of minutes to decide between strawberry and chocolate chip. What was the point in being alive if you couldn't be a little foolish once in a while?

Buying things was distracting, but the thought of Larry invaded them on the homeward bus ride — Marty had to pay full fare, she had forgotten that Juan had her pass — so they stopped at Mama's to see if there was any more news. Nothing, Mama said, but would they sit down and have some cold tea? Juan was going to take her to the hospital to see Larry, so he must be feeling better if they were letting him have visitors.

Stripping for bed, grateful she could sleep raw so she didn't have to wake up feeling smothered and sweaty, Marty said, "I don't think I can stand another day like this one."

"You can stand whatever you have to." Thea didn't feel like making love. Loving, sure. She wanted to crawl inside Marty's skin and lie so close they couldn't tell which was which, but she didn't want to be excited — she wanted to be comforted. Marty hugged her, feeling the same way. She lay thinking about Juan, trying to sleep in the twin bed where he and Larry were usually crammed together, and it seemed greedy of them to have each other when he was so alone. Maybe this is a kind of love, too, Marty thought. As if she and Thea — and Mama and Rico — were all part of one person and they were all Larry.

Like everybody was part of something, like one person.

It was three days later, his fourth day in the hospital, that they found out what was wrong with Larry.

His lungs were clearing, his fever was down, he was having soup and jello, he would get over this unseasonable bout with pneumonia. But they had given him more tests, and he had come out positive on one of them.

Larry, they were told, had AIDS.

Chapter 12

In September Marty found a three-week job in a small downtown restaurant. The owner's wife, who was also the cashier and bookkeeper, had worked out a complicated schedule that allowed one temporary helper to replace three full-time waitresses on serial vacations. It worked, partly because this was a family business and there was no pride of position; Mrs. Sanchez herself wasn't above picking up a broom and sweeping out if the half-witted old uncle failed to show up at closing time. Marty was supposed to wait on customers and help in the kitchen as needed. She had never done any of these things before, but thought, I can fake it, I'm a fast learner. She had learned the computerized registers at Burger Palace, hadn't she?

Thea figured it out. Six hours a day, six days a week at legal minimum, plus tips, which were impossible to estimate ahead of time. "Never mind the tips. That's a hundred and twenty a week. Say they withhold a fourth of it —"

"I don't think they withhold if you're a temp."

"Say they did, you'd have ninety a week, and there's my welfare check. We'll be rich. We'll buy some nice pajamas for Larry."

Marty learned a great deal in three weeks: how to take four orders at a time and keep them straight in her head, how to tell when the construction workers were being abusive and when they thought they were being funny; how to figure sales tax on the checks, when to refill the coffee cups, and how to look as if she understood when a customer ordered in Spanish. Since the rest of the help were already bilingual and had the best kind of job security (second cousin to the boss), someone would translate for her when she got back to the kitchen.

She learned about backaches, how to carry a loaded tray, and about feet — to soak them in hot water when she got home at night and to sit down during the day when business was slow. She took some of her tip money to J.C. Penney's and bought a pair of old-lady black oxfords with medium heels.

She learned to fill the ketchup and mustard dispensers and the chrome napkin holders when she had a free minute, to wipe off the table and set up for the next customer without missing a motion, to run for a damp cloth when some kid knocked over his chocolate milk, which happened about once a day.

She learned about tips. If two waitresses served one customer, the tip went to the one who took the order. Construction workers, from the new skyscraper going up a block away, were good tippers and great kidders. If you kidded back, they would pull out the wallet and show you the snapshot of their kids. It was because of them Mrs. Sanchez had put the sign in the window instead of getting along with a smaller crew; men with one hour for lunch don't like to spend it waiting for service. On the other hand, old ladies who came in for something sweet, a sundae or a Danish and coffee, didn't tip much but they were friendly and liked to chat a little, especially the ones who lived alone. Their snapshots were mostly of grandchildren.

She realized she didn't have to ride home on the bus with a pocketful of dimes and quarters weighing her down; whenever business let up she could run down the street to the bank and trade her tips in for folding money. She was working from eight to half-past two, with half an hour for her own lunch; the place did a big noonday trade and was pretty brisk at morning break time, and her tips came to about five dollars a day. She and Thea hadn't counted on that when they figured her take, and they decided to save the tip money, plus as much as they could of her basic pay. At the same time, they were going to have a few things, including a brand-new washtub; the mail-order houses still sold them, though not at grandma's prices.

Away from the restaurant her life fell into a simple pattern. Thea kept busy all day, although Marty couldn't imagine how she filled the time. She cleaned the house, shopped for food, washed out their socks and underclothes and hung them on the backyard line, to drip on the garlic and epazote plants and the wizened little barrel cactus someone had given her. Twice she went with Rico for the food box pickup, once for the cheese and butter handout — real butter, she marveled. She went to see the Ruizes every day and sat talking with Larry, who was up but not feeling very energetic. She read a lot, not bosomy historical romances now but more books about women's liberation, novels about lesbians and a book called *When God Was a Woman*. The title scared Marty, who had never felt too friendly toward God, but Thea explained that was the "mean, unfriendly, punishing old Yahweh" that men had invented. If you could believe in the Goddess you could believe in love and joy and not feel guilty all the time.

"But read it. It's what people used to believe before they made up all this blood-of-the-lamb shit. It's in the Old Testament. You ought to read Mary Daly, too."

Marty was no reader. If someone left a paper on the bus she read the comics and maybe the headlines, and brought it home for Thea to read and pass on to Larry.

They had supper around five-thirty. Marty got a solid meal at noon, unless business was too good, and Thea ate something when it was convenient, usually with a book on the card table in front of her. At night they had rice and beans, or beans and chili, or something from the food box.

Marty said, "I guess some people would think we shouldn't take the food boxes, but they just don't know the score. Poverty line for one person is somewhere around six thousand. We've got less than half of that, for the two of us. Besides, if we give up food boxes, when I lose my job, we're sunk — it's like welfare, if you go off you can't get back on."

They stacked the dishes and walked down the street to see Mama and the boys. Larry liked to hear about the restaurant, the people who came in and the funny things that happened. Sometimes a few neighbors came in to see how he was doing. Sometimes they brought cookies, and there was always sun tea, which everybody made all year round.

Larry had offered to leave when he came home from the hospital, but Mama said, "Don't be stupid, where would you go?" or words to that effect — it sounded a lot more emotional in Spanish, and Juan said, "If he goes I go too." And where could they have gone? Larry had no money and no job and not much energy, he could just about make it to the bathroom and back to bed, and people with rooms to rent weren't looking for penniless guys with AIDS.

Thea said, " 'Home is the place where, when you have to go there, they have to take you in.' That's a poem," and she tried to put it into barrio Spanish, which made Larry laugh. Not at the evident but at the Spanish.

Juan said, "Don't talk foolishness, man."

Sometimes they talked about AIDS. Thea had

looked it up in the library, in something called the *Periodical Guide,* and it was surprising how many magazine articles had been written about it. The TV preachers on Mama's small black and white set said it was God's punishment on queers — mean old Yahweh again, Thea said — and the gay magazines were urging scientific investigation, since the tests were no way accurate; the manufacturers of condoms were cashing in on the push for safe sex and the managers of baths and cruising bars were frantic. Thea said you could get it from a blood transfusion or from sharing a needle — thank goodness neither of the Ruiz boys was a user — and she said it wasn't that contagious. You had to make love, or swap some kind of bodily fluids — "I'll spit on you," Larry warned, laughing, and Marty hugged him.

They watched the evening news at Mama's. Would Reagan invade Nicaragua? "Man, you hear those Air Force planes every day, going out to the bombing range. They're gonna get the damn Contras to kill all they can, then we'll go in and finish them off," Juan said.

"Six million people in Nicaragua," Thea said, "that was about as many as in Chicago, and half of them were kids."

Marty said, "I'd like to go down there and help."

"What could you do?"

"I could cook."

"You can stay here and cook for us queers."

Would any more cabinet members resign? Would taxes go up? Would the price of salsa go up? Mama wanted to know, but Thea didn't have an answer for that.

"Lesbians are the safest people," Larry said, back with AIDS again. "I heard it on the radio." Marty had bought him a small radio with headphones at the Sallies store, and he listened to it hour after hour when there was nothing else to do.

"We don't play around like you guys. But where do the straight guys get it?"

"What straight guys? They experiment a little — 'What is this gay stuff? How does it feel?' They go home and infect their wives. You dykes have it made."

Juan slept in, or on, a sleeping bag on the floor beside Larry's cot. If Larry woke in the night, scared or wanting a drink of water or something, he was there. Thea said, "There's a word for Juan. *Steadfast.*"

There was no denying that Larry had played around. All those pickups in Times Square, all those tricks in the washroom of the Greyhound Station, all those one-night stands, starting when he was about sixteen. He could have picked up the virus from any of them, and passed it on to others. Juan said he himself had mostly fooled around with kids in high school, but "if I get it, I get it."

Marty didn't know if she would have been that brave. Would she stay with Thea if Thea had AIDS? She felt closer to Thea than she ever had before, but then, she also felt closer to Mama and the boys. If she woke in the night, which didn't happen often, she reached out to touch Thea on her side of the mattress. They weren't making love these days. Marty was too tired when she got home from work and early September was unseasonably hot this year, more like July. The thermometer had hit 110 a couple of days. Their swamp cooler pulled in hot air and sent it out through the front window still warm.

Maybe it was like being married. Marty had noticed that it didn't take long for married couples to get used to each other. The excitement wore off and you were tied down, with kids to raise and a house to pay for. The honeymoon was over. Even couples who lived together for a year or two found it was different once they were married. Maybe she and Thea were sort of married, even though they hadn't gone through any ceremony or made any promises.

In three weeks she learned a great many things she would probably never use again. Mrs. Sanchez took down her name and telephone number — the mama-papa store's telephone number — when she left, and said she would call if they ever had an opening, but Marty knew if that happened another cousin would make it across the border and automatically be added to the payroll. Still it was nice to part on friendly terms.

They didn't make love more than twice during her three weeks of working, and then it was all right, but there was no magic in it. The weather was too hot and Marty was too tired. Thea, alone all day and with plenty of time to think things out, started it, and it was all right, but that crazy excited feeling wasn't there. It was exactly like being married.

Maybe Thea could find a book that would have the answer, but Marty wasn't about to suggest it. In the first place, she didn't want Thea to think she wasn't perfectly satisfied with what they shared, and then she didn't have all that much confidence in books. What little she knew she had learned from real life.

In books, mothers were wise and gentle and loving, ready to sacrifice for their children. Hers had been drunk most of the time, married to a no-good, stayed out late nights and smacked Marty when she felt like it, whether she deserved it or not.

In books, girls discovered love when they were seventeen or eighteen, married some nice young man with a good job, and lived happily ever after. In real life your stepfather sneaked into your bed when you were asleep, shoved his thing into you, and told you he'd kill you if you told your mother. Don't tell anybody, he said. As if she had anybody to tell. The teacher didn't like her, and her mother would have walloped her for lying.

She thought about Joan sometimes, in that lazy time before falling asleep. Cool and self-assured, Joan wasn't so much that she would have liked for a lover as what she would have liked to be; everyone needed somebody to fantasize about and Joan would do. She thought about Joan's primary lover, whose name she couldn't remember, and wondered if she minded Joan's picking up other women. Would a few affairs on the side make a relationship better? She fell asleep before she could answer that.

And in the background was the thought of Larry, who had spent his life looking for sexual excitement and now was going to die because of it. Any little infection, any little change in his body chemistry, and he was going to be wiped out.

It was enough to turn a girl off for the rest of her life.

She had hoped the job would last longer than three weeks — maybe someone would quit, or something — but Mrs. Sanchez pink-slipped her at the predicted time, taking down her telephone number — the number at the mama-papa store. "I will call you if we ever have an opening." But Marty knew if that happened, another cousin would move across the border and be added to the payroll. Still, it was nice to part on friendly terms, and Mrs. Sanchez had put an extra two dollars in the envelope.

Chapter 13

She came across the deposit slip when she cleaned out her wallet. There it was, along with a couple of rent receipts, her Social Security card and a little money — a greenish slip of paper with someone's name, street address and telephone number. She had to think for a minute before she knew who Joan Schiller was.

Joan expected her to call, what else? Joan was attracted to her, had gone out of her way to get acquainted, let her know she was available. What else was all that talk about the primary lover and best friend, about not believing in monogamy? At the time she had thought, Sure, nice work if you can get it, but now she knew why Joan had spelled it out so carefully. She was being cruised.

But there was Thea in the center of her life. Even though they had come together by accident, started making love because Thea was curious, and hadn't made any plans for the future, she didn't think Thea was going to like the idea of a triangular relationship. Thea was taking for granted that they were, as she said, an item.

There weren't many people in Marty's life, never had been. When your mother is a lush and your stepfather is a nightmare, you don't belong to any crowd at school. Afterward she had drifted from place to place, holding a lot of badly paid jobs and always trying to forget her childhood, until the pressure was too much and she ended up in the psych hospital. Since then, surviving was a full-time thing. Now that she had moved out she never saw Aunt Susan, who had enough on her mind without sitting around and visiting, and the neighbors were friendly strangers. Except for the Ruizes, of course — she counted Larry as a Ruiz.

Now the pressure was letting up. With Thea's welfare check and Marty's sometime jobs, they had over two hundred dollars in tens and twenties hidden in the frame of a picture on the front-room wall. Their grubstake. You didn't have a checking account if you were on general assistance. Thea had bought the cheap flower print because they could pry the cardboard back off, slip their bills in, fasten down the little clips and hang it again. There was no other place to hide money, no floor boards to pry up, and the mattress was the first place an intruder would look. Anyway, they had a grubstake. It seemed like a long time since Marty had panhandled in front of the supermarket. It was actually a little over four months.

Thea had her welfare account, they had the food boxes, and Marty might find work any time. She was strong and not bad-looking. Staying alive wasn't a full-time worry any more, they were making it.

She wanted something interesting in her life. Thea could get lost in books about the Crusades or God being female, with pictures of potbellied African statues, but she lived in the real world. Why not Joan, who had this strange attraction for her from the beginning and who kissed as if she meant it? It was what she had been waiting for ever since Eileen.

She and Thea didn't have any wedding rings or any kind of a commitment. They had drifted together, and some day they would drift apart. Thea had discovered her woman-ness, had found out that being "differently abled" (you didn't say "handicapped" any more than you said "girl") didn't keep her from loving and being loved, had been meeting women who believed in being assertive. She knew people Marty had never met, the gang that hung out at the women's bookstore. One of these days she would move over into their world and Marty would be left alone.

She was making excuses, and she knew it.

At the pay telephone in front of the mama-papa store she braced herself for an answering machine. She hated the damn things, but she could see they were handy if you were gone a lot. If a machine answered she would hang up before the little beep;

she would take it to mean that someone (Thea's goddess maybe) didn't want her to get in touch with Joan. She could take a hint.

A cool voice said, "Schiller here."

Marty's heart skipped a beat and hurried to catch up. "This is Marty Brown."

"Who? Never mind, I remember. What are you doing this afternoon?"

"Nothing much." She didn't know what else to say. Was she supposed to make the next move? "I had a job, but it's over."

"Are you free this afternoon? I'm going to be down your way." Marty was fairly sure that wasn't true. Why should it be? "Maybe we can think of something interesting to do."

Breathe easy, she told herself, don't let your knees shake. "That would be nice."

"About three?"

It was almost noon now, it was a two-hour drive from Phoenix. Joan wanted to see her *right away.* But she didn't want Joan coming to the house, even if she did think the barrio looked like a village in Provence, wherever that was. There was Thea. She said, not able to think of any better place, "How about the Burger Palace? About three?"

"Or a few minutes after." Joan hung up, Marty stood looking stupidly at the phone, and then hung up.

Now she would have to think up some story for Thea, like a high school kid sneaking out. There was no reason Thea had to know where she was every minute, but they had a habit of sharing plans. "I'm going to the library, be back by noon." "I'm just going to run in and see Larry for a minute." Thea

136

wouldn't understand if she just took off. And of course she didn't know when she would be back.

Or what might happen before she got back.

She didn't like to lie. Of course you have to lie to government officials and employers, but they didn't count. She would have to make up some story for this. Keep it simple. I'm going to see this girl I used to work with. No, then she would have to describe the girl and the visit when she got home, and she didn't have that much imagination. I'm going to answer an ad for a job. That didn't require any detail, you either got a job or you didn't.

"I'm going for a job interview at one."

Thea was sympathetic but not much interested. She said, "Wear your green shirt, you look great in that one," and started stacking dishes. "I'm going over to see Larry. He's down in bed again. I'm going to take him a library book."

"Don't tell the library people, they'll burn the book." They had to joke about the crazy ideas people had, because otherwise they would break your heart. There was the guy in San Francisco who stayed away from the Gay Pride parade because he was scared of breathing the same air with an AIDS victim, and there would surely be some out on the street. Some school in the midwest had closed down because one of the pupils had AIDS. "What do they think the little darlings are doing, fucking in the washroom or shooting up?" Larry had said. And there were stories of fathers throwing their gay sons out of the house, just in case. When a famous movie star died, a woman in the laundromat said to Marty, "It's God's way of punishing queers. They all ought to be in jail." Thanks, Marty thought, but I'll stay on the outside if it's all the same to you. But of course, straight people thought of queers as male. What women did wasn't important.

Thea washed the dishes and took off for the library, her home away from home. It wasn't even one o'clock. By the time Marty had washed up and changed her clothes and found bus fare it was a quarter of two. She wished she could wash her hair. She wished she had some decent underclothes.

She wished she hadn't got into this, but she wasn't going to back out now.

Suppose Joan was just being friendly? Suppose she had some idea like finding a job for Marty? Marty didn't even know what she hoped would happen, much less what Joan had in mind.

The bus was one of the old ones. It rattled and bumped, the air conditioning was on the blink, and the driver was a learner, nervous because a supervisor was in the front seat, watching his performance. With an hour to wait, Marty got off a stop early and made the rounds of the shopping plaza. Shoe store having a sale on sandals, grocery with a few sleepy-looking housewives going in, dime store with a poster advertising Fancy Fudge. Finally she went into Burger Palace and sat down in a booth. The place was almost empty. She nodded to the cashier, whose name she had forgotten, and carried a Coke to her booth. At least it was cool in here, and she could rest her feet.

Joan got there on the dot of three, not in the big truck but in a compact car that looked fresh from the showroom. She looked even better in shorts than she had in slacks, long smooth legs tanned, classy sandals,

138

hair pulled back smoothly and tied with a ribbon. Quality, Marty thought, that's what it is.

Joan said, "Coke? I'll have one too." She dropped her beige clutch on the table and sauntered up to the counter, swaying just enough to look sexy in a refined way.

They made polite talk. "How was your job?"

"All right. It was a temp, waitressing."

"Have you ever thought about looking for office work?"

"I'm not qualified. You can't even be a file clerk any more unless you can use a word processor." Marty stopped, laughed, shook her head. "Well, that's not quite true, but it's getting closer all the time. Besides, you have to have good clothes for an office job."

"Did your roommate find anything?"

"Not yet. She has a lot of applications in."

Small talk between people who don't know each other very well.

Joan fished a piece of ice out of her paper cup, ate it, and wiped her fingers daintily. "Did you have anything special in mind?"

Marty felt her face redden. "Just saying hello."

"Let's find a nice cool motel and say it in comfort." Joan sounded amused, but not in a mean way. She picked up her beige leather clutch, touching Marty's hand lightly. "It's too hot in the park."

Marty followed her out, feeling thick and clumsy and still not knowing what to expect.

The Happi-Time Motel was out on the northwest end of town, in a not-too-fancy neighborhood near the Interstate. "I stay here sometimes when I'm on a long run," Joan said. "It's nothing special, but they have room service. You can have a drink if you want one."

Marty shook her head, looking around the room.

It had air conditioning, not just a swamp cooler, and the air was dry and crisp. There was a translucent shade on the door, letting in light but no hint of what was outside. Marty had never been in a motel; she saw them on TV, in crime movies or stories about illicit love. She admired the smooth nylon bedspread, the deep chair and little lamps but not the Gideon Bible, which didn't seem to belong there. She used the bathroom and noticed the little bars of soap, the sample-size shampoo, shower cap, shoeshine cloth, the strip of paper across the toilet seat guaranteeing, the print said, that it had been sanitized. She said as casually as she could, "It's very nice."

"So are you," Joan said. "Feel like fooling around?"

She had taken off her shorts and shirt, and sat in a tiny pair of panties, her long legs bare to the hip. "You look so serious. Why don't you take off some of those clothes and get cool? I'd like to look at you."

She scrambled out of slacks, tee shirt, bra and not sure she should — panties. Joan asked, "Why do you wear a bra"

"I'm too big."

"They're wonderful," Joan said softly. She took a heavy breast in each hand and jiggled them, as if playing with tennis balls. Then she bent her head and there was the tentative touch of lips, then an insistent pressure, then the strong sucking — then little prickles like needles all around her nipple, the

140

prickle of small sharp teeth. Marty gasped. It hurt, yet she liked it. "Oh, don't stop!" was that voice hers?

She opened her eyes. There was long slender Joan, ivory where a bikini would be, tan everywhere else — her yellowish pubic hair shaved into a heart shape.

She worked over Marty's breasts until the mix of pain and delight was too much to bear. Joan pushed her over backwards, knelt beside her, and began tracing a path downward with a quick hot tongue, across belly, navel, hips, to the patch of dark hair already dampening. Marty was ready, more than ready, opening to Joan's caress. Marty was making hurry-up sounds, little moans and pleas for more, but Joan was in no hurry. She opened the lips with two fingers, went in, deep, deeper than Marty had known to be possible. A finger circled, found a special place and kept moving until the sensation was unbearable.

"Found your G spot," Joan said, increasing the pressure. "Do you like this?"

It had never been like this with Thea. She made love with enthusiasm, but she didn't fill Marty's breasts with pins and needles and she didn't manipulate that special place until Marty stopped moaning and tried not to scream. The feeling rose, grew, ebbed, rose again — rapture after rapture — and then Joan was lying beside her, sucking greedily, and the biggest explosion came and went on and on, unbearably, and there was nothing else in the world except to keep it, and then she was on a motel bed and the woman beside her was smiling down at her, pleased. "Well! Didn't you ever come before?"

"Not like that."

"Now together. Do me, too."

The position that had taken some maneuvering when she first tried it with Thea came naturally, inevitably, with Joan. They flowed together like two bits of quicksilver becoming one, flowing into place like wind blowing or water finding its own channel. Marty's face was in Joan's heart-shaped tangle of fair hair and her tongue was seeking the deepest place in Joan, deeper, deeper, she was fully awake now and hungry for sensation. There was a new urgency in her own hot and throbbing depths. She was starting all over again — *oh God, oh Goddess* — coming again, and Joan heaved convulsively and gushed against her hungry face, and they were totally together.

Satiated at last, hot and sweat-soaked, tired and happy, they fell asleep twined together, the fancy rose-colored bedspread rumpled and soaked under them and their heads on one pillow. Marty woke later, having slept too deeply to guess the passing of time, and saw the square of glass in the door darkened; night had come. Joan leaned over the edge of the bed and picked up her watch from the floor. "Almost seven, can you believe it? Come on, let's shower and then we'll go and get something to eat."

The bed had been the scene for pure passion. The shower was all fun — touching, laughing, washing backs and bellies and closing soap-slippery fingers around soap-slippery cunts and pulling hair, pouring shampoo over each other's heads and laughing with pleasure as it foamed and multiplied. Marty, with thoughts — fleeting ones — of the washtub and the scanty warm water at home, hated to get out of this bathroom. But Joan reached up at last and turned off the water. "Let's eat. I'm starving."

Now that she stopped to think about it, Marty was hungry too. She looked at herself in the mirror. The face under the wet hair looked different, softer, glowing with pleasure. Joan stood behind her, looking over her shoulder. "I'd like a picture of us like this," Joan said. "Next time I'll bring a camera." They dressed quickly. "Two drowned rats," Joan said. "The air conditioning in the car will dry our hair."

Joan walked into the restaurant with her hair wet, as though she owned the place — no, as though she didn't care who owned it. Marty thought she would have walked in just as calmly if she had been stark naked. She herself borrowed bravado from Joan to follow the maitre d' to a table, to be seated, to accept the big red and gold menu and open it. The right-hand column shocked her. The cost of one entrée would have fed her household for a week. Joan read the shock and smiled. "This is my treat, of course. I'm having Shrimp Cavalier. They invented it here."

Marty said hastily, "I'll have it too." For how could she choose, how could anyone choose from all those pages of fancy names and high prices, especially in flickering candlelight?

It came with a creamy sauce full of garlic and spice, marinated artichoke hearts and mushrooms and other things Marty couldn't identify, but the excitement was wearing off now and she was too sleepy to feel hungry. They rode back to the barrio without talking, a cassette playing softly, and the town had that unreal look things have when you half-wake in the night.

"I hope I'm going to see you again," Joan said, opening the car door. She didn't offer to kiss Marty, but trailed a hand across her knee as she got out.

"Sure. And thank you for everything."

"Thank you too," Joan said, smiling a little.

"I mean, you paid for everything."

"I have a smart accountant."

Marty knew she had plenty of money, but she felt uneasy all the same. With Thea she was the strong one, the one who knew where the good resale shops were and how to fix the drippy faucet. Joan had a different kind of strength, the kind that came with credit cards and a wallet full of twenties. It didn't matter. She wouldn't let it matter.

"I've got a long run the first of the week, but I'll be in Phoenix after Thursday. Give me a call, all right?"

She certainly would. It was going to cause all kinds of complications, but she wasn't going to let go of this wonderful thing that was happening to her.

She watched the taillight wink out of sight and then walked slowly into the house, planning what she would tell Thea. *I met this woman I used to work with, and we had a hamburger.* She would have liked to describe Shrimp Cavalier, but there was no way.

Until half-past eight you had a hamburger?

We had a hamburger and sat around talking. That wasn't much better, but it would have to do.

Chapter 14

The house was locked and nobody was home. Marty dropped her key on the card table and knew that Thea had been gone for quite a while; the house had that empty feeling. Her stomach turned over.

Thea had come home, found her gone, worried about her and run out to look for her at the grocery store, the laundromat, the neighbors' houses. No, that kind of panic wasn't like her. Thea had guessed what she was up to, somehow, and had left unhappy and angry. No, her library book was on the table, with a match marking her place; she couldn't stand to see a book sprawled out on its face. Her clothes were still hanging on the bedroom wall and her toothbrush was in its plastic tumbler in the bathroom.

Marty looked for a note, but there wasn't anything. She took the flower picture down from the wall and pried off the back; their emergency money was all there. She locked the door behind her again and walked quickly to the Ruiz house, forgetting to be tired. If Thea wasn't there, they would know where she was.

She was there all right, and so was half the neighborhood. She grabbed Marty and hung onto her as if she might evaporate. "He's in the hospital again. He had a seizure — it was awful. His arms and legs jerked, he couldn't talk, he kept trying and it didn't make sense. He made those awful noises —"

"We had to call two ambulances," Rico interrupted. Where Thea looked scared, Rico looked angry. "The first wouldn't take him, they wouldn't touch him."

"Son of a bitch."

"I pray to God to give them AIDS, or something."

"Son of a bitch," Marty said again. "I heard about nurses who won't take care of AIDS people — but ambulance drivers? Anybody could die."

"It's like the Middle Ages," Thea said soberly. "Leprosy, bubonic plague . . ." One thing about those books Thea was always reading, she could find some meaning in them for what was going on right now.

Mama said something in Spanish.

Rico nodded. "Thea she got mad and called another ambulance outfit, and she told this one he had epilepsy. No problem, they take him to the county hospital. I pray it's not too late."

Thea said, "They'll do some research on it now that straights are dying from it too. Nobody cared when it was just queers. When that nun died — wow!"

Rico said, "You know, me and Estella have split up. Not that we was so serious anyhow."

"I'm sorry."

"Juan took the test. Negative. They say it can take as long as seven years to show up, from the time you get it. But me? I fooled around some when I was a kid, junior high, like everybody, but there wasn't any AIDS then. Estella's being foolish."

"Probably Juan's all right," Marty said. She didn't know anything about it; in Juan's place she would have been hysterical, but she wanted to reassure someone. Mama, maybe. Mama had enough trouble already — a widow at thirty, no money, three kids born to her and the girl ran away from home, dropped out of sight — just about everything that could happen to a woman. Now she was going to lose her older son, maybe. It wasn't enough to have him turn out gay, now he had to wait, maybe years, for a killer virus to take him away from her. How did she stand it?

Mama got up and went to the refrigerator, which was working for a change, and got out the big pitcher of sun tea; she went around the room filling glasses, got one down from the shelf for Marty. Her face was calm, but Marty knew from the slowness with which she moved and the way her hand shook that she was suffering more, probably, than anyone else. And why wouldn't she be? How was she going to get through the next half-dozen years?

Marty and Thea went home in silence, too heavily

147

loaded with worry to feel like talking. Marty was also loaded with guilt. In this closeness she would have liked to tell Thea everything, where she had been and exactly what she had been doing. Thea would be interested; she always was.

Yeah, and she'd be miserable too.

The notions Joan held about freedom and not owning people, primary and secondary and who-knew-how-many lovers sounded good. Thea would have been fascinated by them if she had come across them in a book. Marty wondered how many lesbians went along with all this. In the novels people fell in love and moved in, fell out of love and moved out, had ex-lovers around, complicating things, or got together by threes and fours. You were left with the idea that friendship was probably a whole lot better than love.

Her sleepiness had evaporated in the excitement of what had happened to Larry. She lay awake for a long time after Thea fell asleep, thinking things over and not coming to any good conclusion. She wanted to see Joan again, there wasn't any question about that, being with Joan was like being under a spell, like the people in fairy tales. She didn't have any choice.

The question was, how could she manage? To begin with, what was she going to tell Thea about today? She would have liked to describe the whole adventure in detail, not just what she and Joan did in bed and how it felt, but the luxurious motel room and the candlelit restaurant and the Shrimp Cavalier. (Thea had been cooking rice for supper when Rico showed up, terrified.) Right now they were all upset over Larry's seizure and the paramedics, but Thea might start wondering about her when life settled back to normal.

She was Thea's first lover, but inexperienced didn't mean stupid. It would be smarter not to bring the subject back at all, but she had better be ready to answer any little questions that just casually came her way.

Would she have done it over if God or somebody had given her a chance? Yes, absolutely.

She had never known anyone as glamorous as Joan. Maybe that was a strange word to use about a truck driver, but it fitted. Joan was like someone playing a sexy truck driver in a Hollywood movie. Going to bed with her was like — well, she didn't have anything to compare it to. It was more exciting than anything she had ever imagined. With Eileen she had been scared, and they were always in a hurry; it was like being given a few crumbs when you were starving. With Thea, experimental, affectionate, the orgasms were a sort of bonus. She hadn't known that making love could be so great, Joan played her like a musical instrument. She vibrated to Joan like a harp.

She went to sleep full of guilt and garlic, and woke unrested.

Her mother used to say that the devil takes care of his own. The old girl knew what she was talking about, Marty decided. A few days later the downtown restaurant lost a waitress and called her to fill in. Now she could take an extra day and say she was working.

Mom said, if you say A, you have to say B. Which means, as near as she could figure it out, that doing one sneaky thing means doing another to cover up

149

the first. She didn't like it, but she knew one thing for sure: if Joan called, nothing on earth would keep her from answering.

Chapter 15

In the first days of discovery, Marty had sometimes thought that the best part of making love was talking afterwards. The excitement faded away and you were relaxed, but not quite ready to go to sleep, and you could lie touching each other and talking about anything that drifted to the surface of your mind, some trifle you had seen or heard, or memories of your childhood — one night they started on jump-rope rhymes and came up with more than twenty. Marty hadn't jumped rope since she was ten years old.

Sometimes they daydreamed about the house they would have when they got rich. Marty wanted something posh, a beach house in California with big glassed-in rooms and gardens full of flowers and a view of the ocean. Thea talked about a little house in Vermont, a remodeled farmhouse or an old barn, fireplaces and wood stoves. It was probably a good thing they were never going to have a house — they were lucky to be able to pay the rent on this little abode — but it was fun to plan for a future you knew could never come true. "We'll live in California in the winter and Vermont in summer," Thea said, and that was all right.

Most of the time they talked about everyday things. Thea moved a little so she could speak; her mouth was against Marty's shoulder. "I almost bought something foolish today. A box of pictures."

"What kind of pictures?"

"Old photos. Ladies with birds on their hats. Ladies holding babies in long fancy dresses. Postcards with one-cent stamps on them. I know they're not good for anything, I just like to look at old stuff."

"Why didn't you buy it?"

"They wanted a dollar for it. You know that secondhand store on Fort Lowell, with the satin wedding dress in the window? They don't mind if you just go in and look, you don't have to buy anything."

"My mother had a box of snapshots," Marty said, surprised that she remembered it. "From the twenties and thirties, I guess. The women had boyish bobs and rolled stockings and the men wore hats. She kept my report cards and spelling certificates, too."

"Were you a good student?"

"Middling. I liked school, but I had a hard time getting good grades."

"How come?"

It was a casual question, she didn't have to answer it. She wasn't going to answer it. "I was scared all the time."

"What of?"

"My stepfather. Worried about was he going to sneak into my bedroom and — do things to me. Worrying was almost as bad as when it happened."

There was a short silence. Marty burned with anger and humiliation. Why did she say that? All these years she hadn't told anyone, except the shrink at the hospital, and she clammed up with him after the first time. It hurt too much to think about it.

Thea's voice was neutral. "Happens to a lot of kids. They're just beginning to find out how many."

"Yeah. I didn't know that, I thought I was the only one."

"How old were you?"

"About nine when it started. They hadn't been married very long." Shut up, Marty, she chided herself, there's no point in all this. But she was uncorked now and there was no way to keep the whole miserable story from spilling out. "I told Mom. Kids do tell their mothers when something awful happens." Her mouth twisted. "She was hung over. She said I was lying, it didn't happen, and she'd whip me if I lied again. So I shut up and kept it to myself. Till I was thirteen."

"What happened then?"

"I was scared of having a baby. I knew about babies. A girl in eighth grade got pregnant and her folks made her have an abortion. After I had my first period I was scared twice as bad, so I caught Mom when she was sober and told her again."

"Did she believe you?"

"Sure. She said I'd tempted him into it and if she heard one more word she'd send me to reform school. She didn't want to believe me. She was getting older and she was sloshed half the time, and I guess she was afraid she'd never get another man if he got mad and left."

"There wasn't anyone you could talk to, a teacher or minister?"

"Teachers don't like kids like me. We were poor, we lived in the wrong part of town. I wasn't one of the nice kids. We never went to church or Sunday school either. I didn't know this stuff ever happened to anybody else. I blamed myself. By that time I felt dirty all the time." She stopped, breathing hard; she felt strangled. "I was lucky I didn't get pregnant. I ran away from home when I was fourteen."

"Where's your mother now?"

"How should I know? I never saw her again. I never called her up or wrote to her. For all I know, she's probably drunk herself to death by this time. I got along okay — I was big for my age and strong, I said I was seventeen and got a job in a dime store. I never was interested in men, and I sure wasn't about to get the drinking habit. Then I had a job doing housework, taking care of people's kids, and that tied me down some. I remember the people gave me a string of beads on my birthday — I had those beads for the longest time. Then when the husband got transferred I moved into a furnished room and went to work in a factory, put a little part in windshield wipers."

"You been on your own ever since?"

"Sure. That was, let's see, almost seventeen years ago I left home. Been on my own all my life."

Thea hugged her closer. It was a good hug. "Didn't you ever have a boyfriend?"

"Makes me sick to think of it, letting a man touch me." That was one thing she didn't need to figure out.

Thea said carefully, "Some people think being gay comes from being raped, or unhappily married, or something. I don't know. I think maybe it's in all of us, all women, only most people are afraid of it."

It was time to change the subject. Marty asked, "How about you? Let's have your life story. You got mine — maybe we can make a soap opera out of it. How come you're where you are?"

"I had a stepmother," Thea said. "Not a wicked stepmother like in all the stories, she was nice to me. That was the trouble. I was her husband's poor little crippled daughter that had to be babied and kept from getting tired. My mother died when I was a freshman in high school and after a year or so my dad married again — I can't find any fault with that or with the woman he picked, it was just I felt smothered all the time. I couldn't play basketball or go camping with the Girl Scouts because it might be too much for me. I couldn't try out for the debate team because everybody would feel sorry for me, poor little thing. Okay, I couldn't make the track team but I could play tennis. I'm as tough as rawhide, you know that, but she couldn't see it. I moped around for a couple of years after high school — by that time she had my dad convinced I was too frail to hold a job — then I got this grant and came out here. It's a long way from Jersey and I liked being free. Then the grant evaporated, and that's when we met."

"Looks like we're both orphans."

"I write once in a while, but I'll never go back there, to be smothered in kindness."

"I guess the world is full of orphans," Marty said. "Some of them still live at home with their folks."

"Maybe it's better to make a clean break. It was my stepmother who convinced me I'd never get married or have any kids. Nobody wants to marry a cripple," Thea said with an edge of bitterness. "Now I know people with handicaps, differently abled people, who do everything. One of my friends at the U lives in a wheelchair — she's married to a wonderful guy and had a baby by Caesarian section. Another one was totally blind, studying to be a lawyer, with tapes and all. If they can make it, I sure can."

"Would you like to be married?"

"Not to any guy I ever met. I wouldn't mind having a baby, though. I like kids."

Marty was scared. "Suppose you found a man you liked?"

"I don't expect that to happen, but if it did we'd still be sisters, wouldn't we?"

That didn't satisfy Marty. The idea of Thea in bed with some man made her feel depressed. Considering Joan, she knew she was being unreasonable, but she couldn't help it.

"Never had a date with a guy," Thea said

cheerfully. "No junior prom, no senior prom, no beach picnics. I used to want it all, but not any more. Because now I know I'm a good person, I'm worth loving. Though I've often thought it would be fun to dance — it looks like fun."

"Hell, anybody can dance, the way they do it now. I'll teach you."

Thea's voice was slow and sleepy. "Compared with you, I've never had any real troubles. Only not having a job or any money, that was scary. I don't know what I'd have done if you hadn't come along." She considered that, and added, "I have to go for a review pretty soon, at the welfare place. I hope they'll keep me on."

"It's not hard to stay on, the trick is getting on in the first place. Even with the government cutting down on anything but weapons, they can't just drop everybody."

"You know," Thea said, "it's not my fault or anybody's that we don't have work. I've been reading up on it. It's because society is all messed up. Ever since the Industrial Revolution, that's when they started using machinery instead of making things by hand, there's been more and more people competing for jobs. Now the question is, what happens to all those extra people? Babies don't die like they used to, and old people live longer. Some places, they let the extra people starve. Here they feed them, but not enough to stay healthy."

Marty whispered, "You don't think there's any hope for us?"

"Sure there's hope. Because it's not a real thought-out policy. It's kind of accidental. Some people do get food — we do. Some get medical care.

We got Larry into the hospital, didn't we? We sort of take care of each other and we learn to get along without all that stuff in the TV commercials. It can be done."

Marty felt as though a heavy load had rolled off her, only to be replaced by another. This new burden wasn't all hers, she shared it with a million other people. She rolled over and shut her eyes, feeling Thea warm against her back.

I'll buy her those pictures, she thought sleepily. I'll even look at them with her.

Chapter 16

Getting away for an afternoon with Joan turned out to be no problem at all. Thea's grant didn't come through, but she got a job from one of the index cards tacked up in the laundromat. A Mrs. Sullivan needed someone to look after her three preschool children five days a week while she was at work, legal minimum from half past seven till four, and she was willing to pay under the table; in fact it was her suggestion. The job was tiring — looking after the children turned out to include marketing, cooking and doing some sketchy housecleaning as well as keeping three lively kids safe and entertained — but she liked them and she sympathized with Mrs. Sullivan, whose husband had left without leaving a forwarding address. Thea was happy to be bringing home some money. "I'm going to take them to the zoo on Saturday," she told Marty. "You want to come along?"

"Sure, why not?"

"They're nice kids. I wouldn't mind having one sometime, if you didn't have to go to bed with a man."

"Artificial insemination," Marty suggested. "Or we could adopt one. I read where two lesbians adopted a little girl. We'll adopt one when we get our beach house in California."

"Our saltbox in Vermont. We'll be rich enough to have two houses, like the snowbirds."

Marty not only went to the zoo, holding the smallest Sullivan's trusting little hand, she took two dollars from behind the picture and treated them to ice cream cones. "I like the monkeys," was her excuse when Mrs. Sullivan thanked her. "I always was a sucker for monkeys."

The Thursday of Thea's second week with the Sullivans, one of the boys from the mama-papa store came to say that a Miss Schiller had called. She would see Marty at two, same place. She gave him a quarter and went into action, trying to decide what to wear and also trying to decide which she felt more guilty about, cheating on Thea or excited by the prospect of being with Joan. She decided it was about fifty-fifty.

It did occur to her that she might call back and say she wasn't coming. She did have Joan's home

160

number (the deposit slip), but by this time Joan would be on her way and anyhow, she didn't want to call. She wanted to see Joan again and experience all that magic, make crazy love until they were both exhausted and happy together. Nothing would keep her away.

With more than an hour before she had to leave the house, she took her time washing and dressing. This time she would shampoo her hair after they got to the motel, but she warmed water for the washtub and crammed herself into it, looking at her own body with distress — compared to Joan's blonde sleekness she was heavy and clumsy, bulged in the wrong places and didn't know how to walk. With time to spare, she walked to the bus stop after her usual one, moving slowly because it was still hot, unseasonably hot for mid-September, and she didn't want to get all sweaty. She went into the secondhand store, not because she expected to buy anything but because she had leftover time. She had bought the box of photographs for Thea and they had looked at them together, catching some feeling of a day now gone; she was glad she had bought them, and it now occurred to her that she might find a little present for Joan. But everything looked tacky; there was nothing Joan would have wanted.

She walked slowly to the next corner and caught the bus, still thinking what would make a good gift for Joan. She had a billfold as soft as butter, with her initials on it. A ring with a huge chunk of turquoise set in silver. Underclothes from the best store. Even if you could guess what Joan would like, there would never be money enough to pay for it.

Joan was a Burger Palace ahead of her, with a

cup of Coke untouched on the orange-topped table. She smiled a small cool smile as Marty came back without bothering to pick up a drink. "Better get something cool. It's a bitch of a day."

She didn't know the cashier, so she didn't have to waste time in greetings. She put her drink down and slid into the seat across from Joan, feeling somehow let down. Joan raised her paper cup in salute, but didn't say anything.

Joan looked trim and cool and beautiful in another outfit Marty had never seen — aqua, with a tight sweater top. Every hair in place. That air of knowing everything, being able to do anything she wanted to. She was the same person, in the same setting, she hadn't changed. Then have I changed? Marty wondered.

It was the waiting, had to be. Everything would be all right when they were alone and in bed.

She set her drink down, spilling a little. Joan said, "Well, let's get this show on the road. Same place as last time, or would you like to try something new?"

"That's up to you."

"You're easy to please."

It sounded like an accusation. Marty said, "Only when I'm with you," and followed her out of the room, feeling clumsy and undiscriminating. Jake had come out from behind the counter and was looking after them, but she didn't care — he was no longer her boss and she didn't have anything to lose.

Same motel, a different room, the bedspread green instead of fuchsia. Actually, in the southwestern style, each room was a separate little cabin and there was no way to hear the people on each side. Marty wondered how many of them were making brief stopovers for sex, how many whores brought their tricks here, how many rents the owner collected in the course of twenty-four hours. It hadn't occurred to her before. Today her mind was jumping around, refusing to focus on the next couple of hours. Yet she wanted more than anything to be here with Joan.

The dull feeling stayed with her. I walked too far in the sun, she thought, I'm tired.

Joan tipped her back on the bed and undressed her, as if she had been a doll, and their mouths met in one of those long hungry kisses. Marty stopped thinking and gave herself over to the magic.

But the magic wasn't there. Everything seemed the same, felt the same, but the response was missing. Was it possible, then, to go through all the physical motions and feel all the responses in your body, and still have some part of yourself holding back, not given over to the pleasure? Marty's body quickened and pulsed, the love juices welled up in her under Joan's insistent tongue, the circles of feeling widened, but she didn't lose herself until the very end and then the going away was brief and somehow unsatisfying.

This was her, Marty's, body, and it was letting her down. But there was more to Marty than lips and hands, cunt and clitoris. There was something more, and Joan wasn't reaching it. She felt like crying, and smiled instead.

Maybe she wasn't a real person to Joan, she decided as she rolled off the bed and headed for the wonderful shower. Joan didn't really know anything about her. Here they were in bed together — on a bed together — closer than they could have been any other way, and they were strangers. She was a woman's body, and Joan knew how to manipulate her. She might as well have been a vibrator. But she wasn't, she was a separate person.

She showered without thinking about the good hot water and the big soft towels, washed and dried her hair — there was a blow-dryer this time, courtesy of the management — and followed Joan to the car. "We'll try a different restaurant," Joan said. "Tucson is a wonderful town for eating out. Spanish, Greek, Italian, Arabic, anything you want." But Marty had no choice. Her eating out had been limited to Burger Palace, Dairy Queen and the downtown restaurant with its unchanging popular-priced menu.

"Anything but rice and beans." But she saw from the tiny pucker between Joan's eyebrows that she had committed a breach of manners, she had torn a hole in their game of pretend.

They went to a rib place, bluff and hearty old-English decor. Marty left half of her beef and most of the baked potato, wishing she could take them home, but of course she couldn't suggest it even though the well-dressed couple at the next table carried out square cardboard boxes of leftovers. How would she explain it? She refused dessert, which Joan politely suggested.

They didn't talk on the way home. She asked Joan to let her out at the corner, and their goodbyes were brief and without sentiment. Joan had her hooked now, she thought; she didn't need any little flirtatious gestures. There was a polite goodbye kiss, like two women friends parting after a social event.

Joan was like a man who hires a woman for a couple of hours, and she, Marty, was the woman, hired for a motel bed and a hot shower and a rich meal.

Joan, she reminded herself was everything she had ever wanted. Beautiful, generous, a skilled lover. Then why wasn't she satisfied? She wished something had kept her from going, so she could have kept the memory of the first time bright and shiny in her mind.

Goddamn it, she thought, letting herself into the house, sex isn't enough. It's all right, but it isn't enough. There ought to be some feeling in it.

Anyway, Thea was at the Ruizes; not surprising, since so many of their evenings were spent there. She could have joined them, but she went to bed instead, and when Thea came in she pretended to be asleep.

In early October, about the time the weather broke, Mrs. Sullivan was pink-slipped. Thea lost her job. The little Sullivans cried at parting and so did she, partly because she was fond of them and partly because their mother owed her two hundred and sixty-eight dollars. "You'll have it the minute I get it," Mary Sullivan told her, with a worried forehead. "The way it is, I can't even pay for Maureen's school clothes. The stores are on me for the charge account." Thea said, "That's all right," and didn't mention that the employer had outfitted her kindergartner from the best shops in town. Twenty-eight dollars for shoes — ridiculous.

They went back to living on the welfare check and food boxes.

The downtown restaurant had evidently forgotten about Marty. The university was cutting down on grants, except for military research. The federal budget was cutting back on all human needs and the new reactionary governor was chopping everything. Marty said, "I don't understand. The university is doing research *for* the army?"

"Just certain things." Whatever the reason, Thea wasn't going to get any money this year. She would try again, next term.

Marty spooned rice on two plates and piled pinto beans on top. "A complete protein. Look at all the people in Korea —"

"— who would be glad to have beans," Thea finished for her. It wasn't funny.

Larry had another seizure and went back to the hospital. Pitiably weak, he was so thin his bones stuck out. They went to see him, and outraged the nurse by hugging him without putting on gowns, masks and surgical gloves.

The city's artsy-craftsy magazine published an article by a well-known novelist suggesting that AIDS patients be given cyanide capsules and urged to end their miserable existences and the drain on the public economy at the same time. Thea suggested buying a Saturday-night special and shooting the author, but since she had never fired a gun in her life and didn't have any money and didn't know where to find him, she said she would settle for making a wax doll and sticking pins in it.

Marty, eating beans for the third day in a row, looked at Thea across the card table. Was she pretty? No. Her face was too thin, her hair was more dishwater-colored than blonde and needed shampooing (a major project even with the washtub, since the water had to be heated in a pan). But there was something about her. Marty said at random, to break the sequence of her thought, "I shouldn't have bought the jogging shoes, even if they were marked down. If I ever get a job, we'll save every penny we don't absolutely have to spend."

"If it comes to that, I shouldn't have bought all those paperbacks. I could have gone to the library."

"Yeah, you must have spent three or four dollars on books. Big deal. Goddamn it, we're human, we have a right to something of our own once in a while. It's like the guys who cash their welfare checks in the tavern and have a couple of beers, aren't they entitled? Can't they spend their money the way they want to?"

"Not according to the gov."

Marty had paid a visit to the welfare office and been turned down. The man who helped her fill out the forms had looked her over and said, meaning to be funny, "You're a good-looking girl. Why don't you find a guy to support you?"

She didn't back-talk him; they needed the money. But her application was turned down anyway. The new governor, a tight-lipped man whose ideas had been shaped before WW II, was on an economy spree and social services were being lopped on all sides. The poor were poorer; the mentally disturbed roamed the streets, mumbling or shouting; it was called "de-institutionalizing." Government talk was all long-winded, or a string of initials.

"An old lady grabbed me and started yelling at me when I got off the bus this morning," Marty said. "I

167

didn't do anything to her — I didn't even see her until she got hold of me. She almost knocked me over."

"My big worry is that one of us will get sick. We're the only state without Medicaid."

Marty laughed, but there wasn't any humor in it. "I'll try to stay well."

Mama Ruiz had her own system of medicine: squaw tea for sore throat and colds, epazote for stomach upsets, chicken soup, if available, for everything else. Marty said, "I thought chicken soup was Jewish."

"It's universal."

If there was any chicken soup around these days, Larry was getting it, and the chicken was coming from cousins, aunts and neighbors who probably didn't like his lifestyle but accepted him because Juan loved him, and because they had all had troubles of their own, or because they were under obligations to Mama. Larry had soup when there was any. The rest ate beans and rice and whatever was in the food boxes.

"I get goddamn tired of no money, no job," Rico said. They were sitting in the Ruiz yard, which had a real tree, a mulberry imported from out-of-state and planted for shade before mulberries became illegal. "You get this idea when you're a kid, you're going to do better than your old man, you're going to college and get a good job and make a lot of money, drive a big car, take care of your mother. Specially now, when us Chicanos are getting to be lawyers and doctors. Hell, we got a man on the city council, man on the school board."

"So what happened?"

Rico spread his hands; how in hell should he know? "Prices go up. Wages don't. It costs five or six thou every year to send a kid to the university. Even the city colleges charge more than we can afford. Maybe the Commies are right, maybe we need a revolution."

"From what I've read about revolutions, they kill off the wrong people. Besides, how are you going to get people out on the barricades when all they want is to get high? Dope is the best friend the government has, it keeps people from rebelling."

"Americans always think things are going to get better," Marty put in. "I bet every guy who's sleeping in the streets still thinks he might have a big car and a good refrigerator some day."

Thea leaned forward, "Rico, what would you like if you could have your pick?"

"I'd like my brother not to have AIDS."

"Oh God, wouldn't we all!"

A nice guy, and nice guys are losers, Marty thought.

They spent a lot of evenings in the Ruiz yard, partly because of Larry and partly because of the tree. Their own yard was a straggle of nameless bushes, all the gray-green or tan-green of desert plants: a clump of broom, some saltbush, a sprinkle of tiny purple flowers growing close to the ground. Marty had planted some onions but they weren't coming up. Here, Mama's red geraniums in gallon cans bordered the back wall of the house, and there was an old bench and plastic-webbed lawn chairs. And lizards. Marty was fond of lizards, not the big scary ones but the little gray ones that sometimes lay on the front sidewalk in winter, enjoying the sun.

Thea said dreamily, "I wouldn't go back east for anything. If you have to be poor, it's best to be poor where it's warm."

"Gets cold in winter," Juan reminded her.

"Not enough to freeze people. When I was a kid in Jersey City we were always reading about some poor drunk found frozen stiff in a doorway. Here all you get is cold."

Marty said, determined to be cheerful, "Anyway, we already bought warm jackets at Value Valley. Mine's quilted, with a hood. Thea's is more of a sweater, with all different color stripes."

"That was smart."

They walked home, thinking ahead. The days were still hot, but at night the desert air chilled quickly and sometimes in the early hours of the morning there was a wind that sounded like a wailing voice. Thea said, "The Navajo say it's the Old Ones, the Before People. They want to tell us something. I wish I could understand them."

They unlocked the door and felt for the box of kitchen matches on the food shelf. The lamp wick kindled and flared up. Thea lifted on the chimney with careful precision. "I wonder what it would cost to run a wire in here from the front room. Probably overload the circuit."

"I like this nice old-fashioned light."

Personally, Marty would have liked modern lighting, not to mention a real bathtub and running hot water. And a kitchen sink and some cabinets — might as well wish while you were wishing. How about a house in the foothills and a million dollars?

It was still too hot to sleep comfortably, but she visited the bathroom, ran a comb through her hair and washed where she thought she needed it most. She came back to the kitchen letting the air dry her. Thea said, "I like your outfit."

"You ought to have one like it. They're very comfortable."

"Go ahead, tempt me."

Marty leaned against Thea's back and reached around to unbutton her shirt. Her breasts felt cool and solid against Thea's hot back. "It's too hot." Teasing.

"Wasn't too hot all summer."

Thea turned in her arms, pulled off the shirt and dropped it on the floor. Her panties were a wisp of nothing. Marty said, "Damn, I wish I could wear those little bikini pants. They look so cool."

"When we're rich," Thea said, stretching up so her breasts could touch Marty's, "we'll have a fur rug to make love on."

"I'd settle for a piece of linoleum for the kitchen floor. I'm tired of getting splinters when I scrub."

"Might as well wish for something far out."

"Bearskin rug."

"Leopard."

"What's wrong with mink?"

"Too tickly."

"You don't like to be tickled?"

"Not by minks."

They walked into the bedroom together and dropped down on the mattress without turning on the dangling light. The rising moon shed a clear yellow light over the bedroom floor. When a car went past the moving headlights made a shifting glow on the walls. Thea said, "I like our little adobe hacienda."

"I like you." Marty sat up, rocked by the idea

171

that had just popped into her mind. "I really like you better than anyone I ever knew. Not making love — *like.*"

This didn't surprise Thea. With her, loving and liking went together. "All talk and no do," she said with a deep fake sigh.

There were no more words for awhile. Their hands spoke for them, exploring, teasing, testing, recognizing answers. By the time the moonlight moved around to the corner of the wall, no one could have told which body was which, they were tangled so close together. There was no need for talk.

Chapter 17

When you've had a run of bad luck, small pleasures add up.

There was a bottle of dish detergent in the food box. Also a can of green chili salsa, which would break the monotony of the everlasting pinto beans — even cooked with epazote to prevent gas, they were getting tiresome. The detergent would do for shampooing. They carried the washtub into the back yard, heated several percolators full of water and washed each other's hair. Thea took a notion for curls and twisted up newspaper strips to make uneven ringlets. "It looks awful," she said when it was finally dry, "but I like it."

Thea discovered a writer named Mary Renault and persuaded Marty to read one of her books, about being gay in ancient Greece. Marty began to think about applying for a library card of her own. After all, it didn't cost anything.

They went with Rico to the government food distribution and after a couple of hours in line, in the cool early morning, came home with five pounds of excellent cheese, a pound of butter and a box of powdered milk. "Rice and cheese," Marty said. "Rice and cream sauce. Rice with butter."

Thea, who hardly ever complained said, "I'd like a hamburger."

"We'll have it when your check comes in."

This was a switch of roles. Was it true that married people got more and more alike? That they came to look like each other? Thea said, "I hope we look like you and not me."

Mrs. Sullivan came to visit, having kept Thea's address. The minute they saw her they knew that something spectacular had happened to her. She gleamed, she sizzled with happiness. She hugged Marty and handed Thea a wad of bills: three hundred dollars, in twenties. "You owe me two hundred and sixty-eight," Thea told her, and then was embarrassed because it sounded as if she had been thinking about it, brooding over it maybe. "I mean, anyway —"

"Take it, take it. I'm getting married."

"Why, that's wonderful." Marty had never seen anything so great about marriage, but you have to be polite; and who knew, it might turn out all right. "I hope you'll be very happy."

"Oh, we will. The funny thing is, we were in high school together, and we liked each other then." Like anyone else making optimistic plans, Mrs. Sullivan was more than ready to go into detail. "He was a BMOC, played basketball, and was on the debate team. Then we both married someone else and I never heard another word about him. Then a couple of weeks ago I went with my cousin Theresa to this nice little neighborhood bar, just for one drink, you know, and who should be there —"

Thea listened with real interest. "He's crazy about the kids. His wife, may she rest in peace, found out after they were married that she couldn't have any. He has a wonderful job with IBM, he goes out on service calls and fixes the typewriters. He was always handy with tools." She dimpled — yes, she had a dimple in her left cheek, Marty hadn't noticed it before. "So when I told him how bad I felt, letting you go without paying you, and you needing it so bad, and heaven knows I owe you more than money could ever pay for and all the peace of mind knowing the kids were all right —"

They were going to be married in church. Not just church, but the Cathedral, and by the Bishop. "Vince is president of the Holy Name Society. You'll be getting a bid in the mail. And I want you to come to supper Sunday night and meet Vince."

Thea asked, "What can we bring?" and then bit her tongue. Beans. But Mrs. Sullivan said, "Good appetites. Do you like mesquite-broiled steak? Vince gave me a grill. He's the handiest man around the place."

Marty considered looking haughty and saying she didn't care for steak in any shape or form, just to see the look on Thea's face, but she hung onto her manners. "We'd love to. What time?"

They got the details and parted with more hugs. Mrs. Sullivan drove off in, they supposed, Vince's car. Or were they going to be a two-car family?

Marty said, "It couldn't happen to a nicer person."

"We'll have to buy them a wedding present."

"With her own money? Or his, I guess."

"Our money," Thea said firmly. "I earned it, all but thirty-two dollars."

"We'll have to buy it brand-new, in a good store." Marty laid the little stack of twenties on the table and set a salt shaker on them. "What do you wear to a wedding in a cathedral? I've never been to a Catholic wedding."

"Your Sunday clothes."

Since they wore the same clothes on Sunday as on other days, that was no help. "It's a second wedding for both of them, and it's in the morning, so it won't be too formal."

"That's a big help, Thea."

"Dresses, I think, and shoes with heels, and nylons. You can't go to a church wedding without stockings."

"Dresses!"

Thea backed down a little. "Or pantsuits, but dresses would be better."

"We'll never wear them again."

"For two bucks, who cares?"

176

It was obvious that wealth had gone to her head. Marty gave in. "Okay, we'll go down to Fourth Avenue tomorrow."

Thea said a little wistfully, "It's nice to hear about someone having good luck. Sometimes I forget everybody isn't on welfare, or wishing they were."

They made the rounds of the Fourth Avenue thrift shops without finding anything Thea thought was suitable for a church wedding. Finally they took the bus to a resale store near the campus. "It'll be expensive, it's aimed at college students." They came out with a blue number for Thea, a green dacron with a jacket for Marty, both simple. "It's better to be too plain than too fancy," Thea said, rejecting pink with ruffles. They found two pairs of shoes with medium heels, a little large, but that was better than toe-pinching. They bought knee-hi's at the supermarket. "I'm not going to wear pantyhose in this weather," Marty said. They walked into a real store and bought an almost-Tiffany lamp for twelve dollars and had it gift-wrapped. They considered buying a bottle of wine for the Sunday barbecue, but Thea said firmly that enough was enough. That was the trouble with spending money, one thing led to another and first thing you knew you were broke and got behind with the rent. "We've never been late and I'm not going to start now," Thea admonished.

Vince McCarthy turned out to be a tall good-looking man, the kind of dark Irishman whose jaw always looks shadowy because his beard grows so fast. He looked older than Mrs. Sullivan ("Call me Mary, I'm not that old," and they saw that she really wasn't now that she had quit worrying and had something to look forward to). The way the kids

177

climbed all over him promised well for the marriage. "They'll probably have some of their own," Thea said when they had been delivered back home.

"They can afford it. I shouldn't have taken a second helping of steak."

"Don't worry about it. People like to have their cooking appreciated."

"I can hardly wait for the wedding. We're getting so high-class."

Marty went to the dime store and bought a complete set of pink plastic rollers. "Here, give yourself a real professional hairdo for the wedding." They bought Larry a pair of striped pajamas and Mama a new sun tea jar to take the place of the one she had dropped, and paid the rent in advance. It felt good to have a little money for a change. Marty bought hamburger and made a great meat loaf. Thea said, "We're Queens for a Day! Shall I curl your hair for the wedding?"

"No way."

"You can't go with it straggly."

"Hats!" Marty said. "You have to wear hats to a Catholic wedding."

"Not any more. You don't even have to eat fish on Friday. I'll trim your hair."

So there was Marty on a chair in the back yard, a towel around her neck, while Thea snipped off one piece of hair after another, then went back to the first side to even it up. "You're scalping me. I'm going to be bald headed. And since when do Catholics not wear hats in church?"

"They had a good Pope a while back and he said they didn't have to. They don't have to eat fish on

Friday any more either, and some of them have guitar music in church."

It was amazing what Thea learned from her reading, casual as it seemed to be. Marty had supposed that all these things came from going to college, but Thea said no, they don't teach anything really interesting in college, it's all divided into different subjects. (Then why did she keep applying for student loans?) You go to college to get credits so you can get a job. She herself had been studying to be a plant expert, or better yet an agronomist — someone who knows all about the soil and raising things, she explained when Marty looked bewildered. "I'd like to invent better plants and even animals, so people everywhere will have enough to eat. There's enough of everything to go around, they just have to stop wasting it. They have to stop raising things for money instead of use. Like those tomatoes we bought that were so tough we couldn't eat the peel. Stuff has been developed so it can be picked by machinery, it can be shipped long distances and stored for a long time. It's no good to eat, but who cares? Or the milk, they take stuff out and put different stuff in so it's no good."

Marty thought, a little sadly, that it was funny for a woman who wanted to feed the world to be living on rice and beans. Thea shrugged. "It's good food. That steak at Mrs. Sullivan's — Mary's — was full of cholesterol, and the animals it came from were probably full of antibiotics. It tasted good, and it won't hurt us for once, but if you ate it all the time you could have high blood pressure or a heart attack, or something."

Rico said, "You talk like a vegetarian."

Marty blew a stray bit of hair off her chin. "We eat like it, too."

Thea had become acquainted, at the women's bookstore, with two girls — women — who were vegetarians. They wore baggy white pants tied at the ankle, and for a while she thought they were some kind of foreigners, but no, they were from Arizona. They talked about women and their power, the way women are brought up to believe in male values and the way a male-run society rejects them as soon as they start looking for their own way of being. "They might come to see us some day. You'll like them. They believe being a lesbian isn't just sex, it's political."

How much she knows, Marty thought; and I used to think I was the strong one. She said, "Stop scalping me."

"Looks pretty good." Thea stood back to look her over. "A little short, but good. You'll see when I comb it out."

They dressed with great care for the wedding. The outfits they had bought were simple, so it didn't matter that they were probably four or five years out of date. They were classics. "Besides, we'll probably never wear them again." The shoes were a little uncomfortable, but as Thea pointed out, they would be sitting down except for the walk to and from the bus. Thea put a ribbon bow in her curly hair and offered one to Marty. "I'd feel like a horse. Besides, nobody's going to look at us anyway. They'll be looking at the bride. Even the groom doesn't get any attention at weddings."

"His turn comes later," Rico said.

Still, they held back a little when they stepped into the sanctuary. So many lights, so much glitter, lighted candles, holy pictures along the wall — Stations of the Cross, Thea explained later — and so many dressed-up people. They might have left, but two young men with buttonhole flowers came forward and led them to seats about halfway down and in a few minutes there was organ music and Mrs. Sullivan — Mary — came down the aisle beside a man who might have been a brother or cousin, and followed by a sweet-looking woman in pink. Mary wore a cream-colored dress with lace on it, and a little hat. She looked happy enough to have been a young girl in love for the first time. After three kids, too.

And there were the kids in the front pew — Joey in a little white suit, Maureen and Sheila in ruffled matching dresses, looking proudly at their mother. Thea felt proud, thinking how many times she had cooked their lunch and washed their faces. She had smacked Maureen a time or two — she felt almost like part of the family.

Lesbians ought to have something like this, she thought as Vince and his brother stepped forward to meet the bride. Something to remember when things get rough. Did women ever marry each other? Would churches let them? We need a church of our own, Thea thought. They would never let us use the regular one. ("We have *one*," Thea mentioned afterwards, "but they're so Blood-of-the-Lamb I couldn't stand it. We need a church where they worship the Goddess.")

Marty was getting so many new things to think about, she felt confused. She tucked it all into the back of her mind to consider later and sat watching and listening. She forgot her new shoes rubbed her heels, and that they were going to have rice again for supper. Maybe there will be refreshments at the reception, she thought hopefully. Maybe there will be wedding cake for everyone.

Chapter 18

Three weeks later they were in church again, as if the wedding had been a jinx. This time it was for Larry's funeral.

He had died suddenly, in the middle of a third seizure. His arms had lashed out and he stammered something and then fell backward on the bed, looking surprised. Juan was with him, the only one at home. Mama, coming in with a quart of milk from the corner store, sent a neighbor child to the lumberyard — Rico had a day's work unloading and stacking boards — and another to tell Thea and Marty. By the time they got there the house was full of neighbors, everyone talking at once. Someone had brought tortillas, someone was making coffee. Larry would have hated it.

"He's not here to see it," Marty said reasonably, but Thea shook her head, tears running down her face.

There was a lot of fuss. They had to call a doctor, then the coroner, then the county people to make arrangements for the funeral. The man from the county office was polite. They had better have the burial the next day, considering the weather. There was no doubt that Larry was indigent. Larry, or what was left of him, was carried away in a long basket. Mama went with him, and some other old lady, cousin or neighbor or something, they never knew, took over the kitchen and the landlord manned the front door, soberly letting people in. People were already overflowing the house, going to stand in the back yard and wait for Mama's return.

Someone went out and called the priest, not the dignified silver-haired bishop who had married Mary and Vince, but a young parish priest in slacks and a tee shirt and Birkenstocks. Since he hadn't been there to administer the last rites, and Larry wasn't a believer — they were already putting him in the past tense — he thought they might say the rosary. Everyone knelt, except the old lady in the kitchen and the two Anglos in the doorway, Rico wasn't a believer either, but he knelt out of habit or politeness, it was hard to know which. Maybe if you are brought up in a religion, you go back to it in times of trouble.

Juan knelt, but his lips didn't move. He looked as if he were asleep and couldn't shake himself awake.

More people came in the back way with coffee in a plastic bag, oranges and *pan dulce*. None of the neighbors had anything, but if you put enough nothings together they added up to something. Every one of those people knew what it was to be poor, every one knew what it was to lose a loved one. But not many had lost sons or husbands from such a terrible, such a needless disease.

Thea was crying. Marty wished that she could cry, but she only leaned against the door jamb and looked dumb.

She wished Juan could have gone along to the morgue, or wherever they were taking Larry — funeral parlor, probably — as he had gone in the ambulance. Marty didn't know how these things were done, but she felt that Juan should have been there, friend and lover and next of kin. But his and Larry's relationship wasn't allowed. At weddings and funerals you had to disguise yourself, fit into a pattern. When Mama came back from wherever it was she looked for him over the heads of other people, but he stood still and said nothing. The young priest, finished with his prayers, went over and put a hand on his shoulder. If he knew, he wasn't going to speak. At least he wasn't afraid to touch Juan, who might know in five or six years whether he was going to meet the same death as Larry; at least he didn't look as if he thought Juan was a sinner. More as if he were a human being in deep wordless sorrow, and if he, the priest, could do anything to lighten it he would. Maybe some religious people are all right, Marty thought, only how do you find them?

Sometimes she hated all straight people. One thing, she was never going to wear that damned dress again. She was going to be what she was.

She did wear it to the funeral the next day, more for Mama Ruiz than for any other reason. Mama was muffled in black, with a veil that must have gone through a whole lot of funerals. Marty couldn't hurt her feelings by showing up in slacks, though some of the young girls did. Everyone in the barrio seemed to be there, including a lot of subdued-looking little kids.

Since indigent people didn't get the services of a high-class funeral parlor, with soft organ music and potted plants, they took Larry's coffin from the mortuary to the parish church. Larry lay with his head on a flat little pillow, looking like a stranger. There was a stiff little wreath on the coffin, two candles at its head, one at the foot. Thea said afterwards that three was a magic number; the Christians had taken it over but it really started in the old times of phallic worship. That would have tickled Larry. Thea was reading some strange books these days. Marty suspected that she read them by installments in the women's bookstore. She was a fast and retentive reader.

The family and close friends went to the cemetery, crammed into a variety of cars, vans and pickup trucks — no hired vehicles either. It was the poor part of the cemetery, no tall shafts or big fat headstones like the ones they passed on the way in. Some of the graves had little picket fences around them, and on some there were little glass or plastic boxes with photos of the departed in them, shielded from the weather. Some had plastic flowers on them, and some of the small ones had a toy in a plastic-front box. "High mortality rate," Thea whispered, taking Marty's arm as they plodded towards the new grave that was waiting for Larry.

Marty didn't want to think about social problems. She didn't want anything except to go home and sit down.

After the interment, which took about three minutes, the undertaker took the green cover from the grave and rolled it up to use again. He handed Mama one of the carnations from the wreath. She would give it to Juan when they were alone. That was what Juan would have left of his lover, a cheap wired flower and AIDS, unless he was lucky.

They went back to the house and ate tortillas and drank coffee with the rest of the mourners. Thea had cooked up all the beans they had left and brought them in a big bowl. It was two days until food-box time and she didn't know what they were going to eat until then, but there are some things you have to do. The kids, given plates of beans and salsa, went out in the back yard to eat.

"I feel like part of the neighborhood," Thea said as they walked home. "A death and a wedding — no births, thank the Goddess."

Marty looked at her.

Thea said defensively, "Sure I believe in the Goddess. Not that mean old Yahweh, always punishing people. Men invented him to keep women enslaved. It's in the Bible."

"All religions are phony."

"Sort of," Thea agreed. "There's a little piece of truth in the middle of every one, 'cause there's always a few honest people, but they dress it up so you have a hard time finding it."

Everything went back to normal. The men put away their good suits until another occasion came along, maybe a wedding or christening or All Saints' Day. The women had their houses to keep, their babies to tend, their jobs to go to. Fall terms had started at the community college and the young people went off early in the morning carrying stacks of books, to get the education that was going to make them somebody in the world. Learning was the way to get somewhere. There were Spanish names listed in the Yellow Pages under "Attorneys" and "Physicians and Surgeons." Thea said there had always been rich and influential Hispanic people here; Arizona was part of Spain before the yanquis came with their army forts and their businessmen. One of the biggest department stores, closed now, carried the name of an alcalde whose family photographs and fancy clothes and heavy carved furniture could be seen in the museums. Before their day it had been the Indians, the Navajo and Yaqui, the Zuni and O'Odham, called Papago by the Spaniards. Then the Spaniards came across the ocean and built their big cathedral, with the Moorish bell tower and carved arabesques on the front. Last of all came the gringos. "Negro cowboys, too." Thea had read about them somewhere.

Now the ordinary people were sending their children to college, like other ordinary people. Walk around the campus and you saw white, brown, black, Orientals. Thea's pals at the University had been a man from Nigeria and a girl from Hong Kong and a young woman from Sweden. The world was getting more mixed-up all the time.

How had Marty lived there so long and never

188

noticed? Here was this quiet little neighborhood of theirs, only a few blocks from the food co-op and the thrift shops and artsy-craftsy places, and she had never noticed until the search for a cheap place to live brought her there.

The downtown restaurant called her for two days' work and she made about forty dollars in pay and another fifteen in tips. They had hamburger; Thea was beginning to think about becoming a vegetarian, but she liked meat. They bought a pound of instant coffee, not as good for them maybe as Mama's herbal brews but better-tasting in the morning.

Thea filed another application for a grant, put in for a job at the downtown library, and learned from a book how to make tortillas from corn ground in a *metate*. Bits of lime came off the stone and made good bones and teeth, the book said. Mama laughed when Thea told her. "My cousin down there" — waving southward — "she makes." But she hadn't seen her cousin in years, so that was no help. There were no *metates* in the thrift shops.

Thea put a baby-sitting notice on the bulletin board at the laundromat, but nobody hired her.

They went with Rico for food boxes and saw one of the kids who had told them about the place, Aunt Susan's neighbor. He was the only one left of the old bunch, he said cheerfully. Robin died of an OD, Julie went home to her square family, Brian and Chris moved to San Francisco and joined a commune. The old place was still open, new kids moved in every once in a while, though the landlord would have kicked them out if he could have found a paying tenant. "Times are tough," he said, as if they didn't know. "I was sorry to hear about Larry."

"Do you realize we've known each other less than five months?"

"Can't be."

"Middle of June. This is October."

Marty applied for a job with IBM, packing typewriter ribbons. Vince McCarthy put in a word for her, but she wasn't hired. They said they would keep her application on file.

Thea met the two white-pants women again in a bookstore. They had been out on the desert with the Free Amazons, celebrating the autumnal equinox. Free Amazons. Thea knew about Amazons, those warrior women who cut off one breast so they could hold the bow, but these women were intact; she didn't know what they were doing in Arizona in the twentieth century. One of them lent her a book with a proud-looking woman archer on the cover. She started reading bits to Marty as soon as she got home.

"I wish we could buy books. That's what I want more than anything," Thea said.

Marty wanted so many things she couldn't keep track of them. If someone had handed her a million dollars she wouldn't have known where to begin. She had a mental list that included practically everything in Penney's and Sears. (Sears had stopped printing catalogs and she took it as a personal insult, but that didn't stop her from browsing through their retail store.) She hung over the J.C. Penney catalog in the shopping mall; they charged four dollars for it, or she would have read it all day at home. She dreamed of waterbeds, ready-stick linoleum, sheets, Teflon pans, jogging shoes, new slacks and too many other things to list. Meantime, Thea wondered about moonlit rites in the desert.

There was a single ten left behind the picture frame, saved for really dire emergencies.

Thea applied for a job as stock girl in a gift shop, as a hamburger frier in a short-order place, as a door-to-door saleswoman of cheap novelties — ugly little plastic chickens that laid plastic eggs. The gift and novelty people wanted twenty dollars for a sales kit, which took care of that.

Marty answered a blind ad for earning money at home. It turned out to be soliciting orders for dance lessons by telephone. They had no telephone. It would be straight commission, Rico told her, and people slammed the phone down when they found out what you wanted. Juan had bit on one of those ads, once.

They paid the rent out of Thea's November check and didn't have enough left for much else. The food box contained rice and cornmeal but no canned tomatoes, no powdered milk. "I dream about salads," Thea said wistfully. "Big salads with lettuce and tomatoes and cucumbers and little green onions, and Thousand Island dressing."

"I dream about steak, and baked potatoes with sour cream."

"Shut up, you're making my mouth water."

In the middle of all this wanting, the kid from the mama-papa store came with a message for Marty. Joan would see her at three o'clock, same place.

Chapter 19

She did think about not going. By pure good luck
Thea was out of the room when Ray knocked; by
good luck she, Marty, answered the door, but there
was no way she could leave in the middle of the
afternoon and not get back until who knew when,
and not offer some kind of explanation. She didn't
like to lie, and besides, she wasn't very good at it.
But miss seeing Joan? True, the last time hadn't been
what she expected, but she decided that was her
fault, she must have been tired or something.

"Job interview," she told Thea, who was tearing

the sheets off the mattress, getting ready to go to the laundromat. "I might be late getting back."

"Great. What's the job?"

"Assembly line." It was all she could think of. She would be out for several hours, she would have time to think up some convincing details before she got home. After all, she wasn't *married* to Thea. She could spend some time with a friend if she wanted to.

Last time was the wrong time of the month, or something. She hadn't responded well, she hadn't let her feelings take over the way they did when it was really good. Joan had probably been disappointed in her, though she was too nice to say so. This time she would forget everything except the wonderful exciting feelings that Joan's hands and lips invented in her, the deep, deep fire and flood, the nothing-else matters. She looked around guiltily, feeling the want begin, feeling her crotch dampen. She would remember that she had to do her share.

There was a phrase Thea had used once, "recreational sex." That was what this was. No strings attached, no holds barred, just fun for both of them, and deep satisfaction. She didn't really want anything else.

She and Thea hadn't made love much, lately. They were still feeling sad about Larry and worried about Juan, and they were too worried about money to fix their minds on anything else. Would the rice hold out till food-box day? Could they afford a quart of real milk? What would they do for soap when this bar was gone? How did she replace the worn out sneakers? And Thea was gone a lot in the daytime, making new friends who were feminists and Amazons — poets, too, some of them — and when she was at home she always had a lot of discoveries to talk about, but none of them seemed to lead to bed. Thea's adventures these days were mostly in her mind, and Marty tried to follow where they were taking her. She didn't always understand the things that excited Thea, and she tried not to feel jealous of her for being so smart. By the time they got to bed, they were usually too sleepy.

She went through her skimpy stock of underwear and tee shirts from the cardboard box where she kept her clothes, and found one decent pair of slacks. You look as good as you can for an interview, don't you? While she was combing her hair Thea came into the bedroom with a handful of small change. "Bus fare, and get a cold drink or a coffee if it's a long one." Marty took it, although there was almost no money in the house and this would have bought a loaf of bread, or taken Thea to and from the library. It took all the determination she had to hang on to her intention — she *would* meet Joan, she would take whatever Joan had to offer. The look on Thea's face, so full of innocence and love, made her feel like throwing up.

Thea stood in the doorway watching her walk towards the bus stop. Marty wished she would go inside.

It was autumn now. The cicadas, which had been tuning up all summer, sang in every empty lot and dried-out front yard she walked past. The sky was a clear bright blue. Tourists said there were no seasons here, it was summer twelve months a year, but she knew better. Autumn had a soft mellow quality, even though it was warmer than those of her midwestern childhood. The winter would be cold and crisp in the morning, warming as the day passed, and the winds would wail around houses. She had wondered sometimes whether she would go back to Indiana, supposing someone offered her a job there, but what was there to go back to?

The farther she got from home, the better she felt. It should have been spring — she hadn't felt so young and full of juice in a long time. There used to be a song, "It Might As Well Be Spring." That was a long time ago, but she remembered it from somewhere. There was another one, "Younger Than Springtime Are You." She was beginning to feel that way.

She had a right to make up her own mind, didn't she? She and Thea had been together too much, and while there weren't many decisions to make — they mostly did what they had to do — they talked things over. Shall we have rice or beans for supper, or both? Now if someone had given them the choice between steak and fried chicken, that would have been worth discussing. She'd been a loner before Thea came along; now it felt good to be on her own for a while. Or was she kidding herself, trying not to feel guilty?

She stood on the corner spinning a little dream, a house of her own, nothing rich or wonderful, just a house, and a woman — what would she look like? — meeting her at the end of the work day. Was that so much to ask?

The palo verde trees in front of Burger Palace looked wilted and faded. It was fall, all right.

Joan was there before her, sitting impassive at a small table with a cold drink in front of her. Marty said breathlessly, "I'm sorry if I'm late. The bus took a long time." Joan didn't answer. But of course bus schedules didn't matter to people like her — they got in the car and took off to wherever they wanted to go, paid for the gas with a credit card. People who mattered had cars with pushbutton windows and air conditioners, and traded them in when they stopped looking new and shiny.

People who mattered never went into resale shops.

Joan said, "Let's get the show on the road," and stood up in that fluid, all-one-piece way she had, that made Marty feel clumsy and too big. Marty wished there had been time for a cold drink; her throat felt dusty. She followed Joan through the parking lot and got into the car, noticing that Joan's breath smelled of alcohol — she had probably had a drink with her lunch, nothing wrong with that. But Marty had never known her to take a drink; the two dinners they had shared, she ordered coffee with the meal. Well, it didn't matter. She wasn't a lush like Mom, she could drive after a drink or two. It was just that the smell stirred up memories Marty would rather not have had.

They were hardly inside the motel when Joan said briefly, without so much as a welcoming kiss, "Undress."

Marty stared. The other two times, undressing was a game. They did it together, pulling off each other's clothes, with kisses and touches and little nibbles in between. That was part of the pleasure. A sort of appetizer leading up to the moment when they would fall on the bed together and feel the excitement rising and taking over.

She looked inquiringly at Joan, but Joan's face was blank. As if she were a robot, Marty thought. Only her eyes narrowed a little. She said, "You dumb bitch, I said undress. What's the matter with you, can't you hear?"

"But — but —"

Joan's fist caught her on the point of her chin, making stars explode in her head.

It hurt more because it was so totally unexpected. She staggered backward, managed not to fall, and found herself clutching the edge of the bed for support. Joan stood looking at her with an expression she had never seen on anyone, not even on Mom when she was too drunk to make sense. Mom hadn't hated her. She wouldn't have been surprised if Joan had pulled a knife or a gun, like somebody on TV.

She had to get out of there.

Joan said in an icy voice, "Snotty little tramp, aren't you? I can pay for everything, the motel and food and all, and you're still too good to do what I say." She swung again. This time Marty saw it coming and ducked. Joan fell across the bed and lay there glaring at her.

The door was pushed open from inside. A small fair-haired woman stood against the sun glare, looking determined and not at all surprised. "Go," she told Marty. "Just go. I can handle her."

Joan got to her feet, scowling. Marty stood, unable to move. "I don't know what happened," she said stupidly.

"Coke," the woman said. "Coke and vodka. It's a bad combination. I'll get her into a cure if it's the last thing I do. Why don't you go away?"

"I don't have any way to get home." She didn't know where she was, she hadn't paid any attention during the drive here, this time or the other times, and didn't know where to find a bus or what bus to

197

take; and the blow on the chin had left her a little dizzy, or maybe it was the shock, everything happening so fast.

The woman unzipped her clutch purse and peeled a bill off a stack of them. "Take a taxi. There's one in front of the office."

It was very hot for October, Marty's jaw hurt and she felt unreal. She stumbled out of the little room and found the office — a big sign in front of it — and sure enough there was a taxi. A Yellow. She got in, slammed the door, and gave the man her address. He looked unconvinced. Of course, he didn't get many fares from that part of town. She waved the bill at him — a twenty — and he started the engine with a roar and they were off.

The motion of the car restored her reason, more or less. She looked curiously at the buildings they were passing, big houses lavishly landscaped in the southwestern way, with cacti, aloe vera and palo verde in careful arrangements. They passed a shopping mall with new-looking modular buildings. She was going to need that twenty; she had been taken a long way from home, in more ways than one.

The meter had clicked off more than fourteen dollars by the time they pulled up in front of the house. She said, "Keep the change," and went in, moving slowly because suddenly she was tired all over.

Thea stood up when she came into the kitchen, as if she had been waiting. She put her book down without marking the place. "Wow. What happened to you?"

She had supposed that being slugged was the worst thing that could happen to her. Now she knew better. The worst thing was the look on Thea's face.

Her mouth was beginning to hurt. That was more of a wallop than she had supposed. She said, "A woman I was with —"

"I think," Thea said, "you'd better start at the beginning and tell me the whole thing."

"She used to come to the Palace." Marty stopped and tried to arrange her sentences, but there didn't seem to be any good way to tell this. "She drives a truck but she's not a diesel dyke — she's smooth, like somebody in the movies. She was drunk." She heard herself being aggrieved, complaining. "She was never drunk before."

"And you came home in a taxi. Look, all I want is the truth. Just tell me what really happened."

"Some woman followed us to the motel. Her lover, her keeper, I don't know what she was. She gave me a twenty and told me to get out, said Joan was on coke and vodka — my God." "Coke," which at first she had taken to mean Coca-Cola, now took on a scary other meaning. "That's why she always seemed so cool. She was high."

Thea said, "All right, I believe you. It would take Hitchcock or Mickey Spillane to make up a story like that. How many times was always?"

"Three. This would make three."

"Do you love her?"

"I don't know," Marty said truthfully. "I was sort of dazzled by her. It was like I was dreaming."

"You're awake now," Thea said in a voice Marty

had never heard her use before. She marched into the bedroom and began taking her clothes from the cardboard box.

Marty followed her. "What are you doing?"

Thea folded her pajamas and laid them on the bed, folded a pair of jeans and laid them on top of the pajamas. "Moving out. I wish I'd never moved in."

Marty couldn't find any good answer. "I wish you wouldn't. I can't get along without you."

"That's what you think." Thea added two shirts to the pile, went into the bathroom and came back with her toothbrush, and dumped the smallest of the cartons so she could pack her stuff in it. She walked into the front room and took down the picture. The single ten-dollar bill looked small and worthless. "I'm leaving you the ten, but I want the picture. It's mine, I picked it out. Souvenir of a dumb relationship."

"Why?" She meant, why are you leaving, and Thea knew it.

"I knew something was going on, but I didn't think you were so dishonest — so phony. I love you, I guess, though how would I know? I just don't trust you or respect you."

"Where do you think you're going?"

"I know where I'm going. Rollingearth and Mountaintop will take me in for a while."

She walked faster than Marty had ever seen her walk, limping hardly at all and carrying the box as if it had no weight. At the door she stopped. "Let me have enough change for the telephone. I gave you all I had."

Marty gave her a quarter and watched her go

down the street, carrying everything she owned in a grocery carton. She wanted to cry, but she couldn't.

It wasn't until much later that night, almost morning, that she realized what had happened. She had not only lost Thea — and how was she going to live without Thea, what did she have that was worth living for? — but she had no money, no job, no welfare coming in. The welfare check was Thea's. Thea had been supporting her. A ten-dollar bill was all that stood between her and hunger.

Chapter 20

Rico said, "I always thought you guys were monogamous. Women are, mostly."

Marty shoved her food box onto the back seat of the car and shifted it to make room for his. "Shows how much you know about it. Anyhow, we never talked about it. With us, everything just sort of happened."

Rico cleared his throat. "What you going to do now? I mean, you had Thea's welfare check. You need to apply for your own account."

"I tried that."

Now he would say, "Try again." But he didn't. He said, "They're cutting down on everything. Health care. All the crazies are out in the street. Nothing for nobody with this new governor."

"Damn the governor," Marty exploded. "Damn Reagan and the Congress. What do they care? People are human, people have a right to food and a place to live, don't they? This is supposed to be the richest country in the world."

"Only for some people. They don't need so many people anymore, they do everything with computers. There's always going to be more people than jobs. That's why me and Estella busted up. She wants kids."

"Don't you like kids?"

"Sure. I'd like a dozen. Only who feeds them, who buys shoes for them? You think it's easy to find a job when you're Chicano? It's ten times as hard as for Anglos." He caught her unbelieving look — hadn't she tried, with no luck? "I wanted to have that operation, you know, where you can't make babies but you can still make love. She couldn't see it. Mexican men, they're proud of their families. I can't blame her."

Marty didn't have any answer, and she was tired of talk. Seemed as though everybody talked and nobody did anything. She climbed into the passenger seat. "Okay, I'll go back to the welfare office. Maybe if I look tacky enough and act real meek they'll put me on."

They didn't. There was nothing personal about it, the woman at the office assured her, as if that made things better. Federal funds had been cut, state funds were limited; personally, she would have liked to help everybody who deserved it, but they had to give priority to people with children. Marty nodded; she couldn't fault that. "You're a good-looking girl, why don't you find yourself a husband?"

Marty said, "If I have to make my living that way, I'll go out on Oracle and lean against a lamp post." She walked out, turning her back on the surprised worker.

That took care of welfare.

She signed up with two temporary agencies, the kind that get short-term low-pay jobs in stores, fast-food places, small offices. Slave markets. There were others along Broadway and Stone that found jobs for men on farms, ranches, construction sites, the signs advertised, "by day or week," but they had nothing for women. Since the Sanctuary movement started it was harder for wetbacks to get into the country, work a few months and go back to Mexico with savings against the inflation. Ranchers had depended on wetback labor ever since Territorial days, and the border guards turned a deaf ear and blind eye. Now the border guards were looking for Guatemalans, Salvadorans, people from Nicaragua fleeing the horror of the Contra death squads, and since they couldn't tell one Hispanic accent from another they also screened out the seasonal workers.

Anyway, there were no ranch jobs for women. They worked on the truck farms, alongside their husbands and parents, but they didn't solo.

A little Thai restaurant down the street from the welfare agency had a hand-lettered sign in the window: DISHWASHER WANTED. She went in, but they had already hired someone. Anyway, they probably wanted a man.

She went home and ate some beans. There was food in the house, she probably wasn't going to starve, but how was she going to pay the rent? A hundred dollars was nothing — she would never find another place for so little. Mrs. Sullivan — Mary — had paid three-forty for a two-bedroom house, cramming all the kids into one double bed. A hundred dollars was nothing, it was just that she didn't have it.

She called Aunt Susan, who was glad to hear from her but opened the conversation by mentioning, carefully-casually, that she had rented her little room to a nice steady young man who worked for the Post Office. That was another door slammed in her face.

When she and Thea joined forces, she was the strong one. Or thought she was. Hadn't she supplied a place to stay when Thea was frightened and powerless? Wasn't she the one who knew how to fill out forms, where the welfare offices were, how to get along in the world without money? Hadn't she bummed change in the shopping center when Thea needed bus fare? (Looks like I'll be doing it again, she thought grimly; more competition now.) Thea was a scared little tag-along, a refugee from the middle-class world. But it was Thea's welfare check that had kept them going; and she was the one who knew *why* things were the way they were. She knew about politics and the cold war; why Star Wars wouldn't work and why women were paid less than men. Thea was smart, and it had nothing to do with having gone to college.

Thea would have known there was something wrong with Joan, and even if she hadn't, she would never have sneaked around behind her lover's back for the sake of all that phony glamour. She would have talked it over.

Thea knew things. Bookstore, library, neighborhood house things. *Neighborhood house.* Weren't they supposed to do things for poor people?

She counted her change, found enough for bus fare, and headed for the place where they gave away the federal surplus food. Now don't expect anything, she warned herself as the bus jolted along. If they had jobs to give away, someone in the neighborhood would know about it. But what the hell, she couldn't sit home and worry, she might as well get turned down one more time.

She didn't really know what neighborhood houses were supposed to do — help the poor and backward to get along, or teach people things they needed to know. Thea had said something once about taking Spanish lessons, but nothing had come of it, they were always too busy and it was quite a trip by bus. She had a mental picture of aging spinsters with sour faces handing out good advice. Still, she was willing to give it a try. At least they probably wouldn't tell her to get married.

What she found was a skinny young man in shorts and sandals overseeing a basketball game in a bare room that might have been a gym or auditorium or meeting room, and probably was all three. He listened for a minute, one eye on the kids, and nodded. "I know what you mean. There isn't anybody in right now, though — you didn't have an appointment, did you?"

Marty said, "No, and I don't have an appointment to get hungry, I don't have an appointment to get thrown out of my house either, and I'm sick and tired of all this welfare shit." She felt better. She had killed any chance of getting helped, but she sure did feel better.

"I'll drink to that. Sit down, why don't you, and I'll bring you a Coke. That won't help, but it won't hurt either."

The game over, the kids scattered. The young man went into the next room and came back with two frosty cans of Coke. "What have you been doing?"

"Waitressing. Assembly line, but there isn't that much industry in Tucson. Baby-sitting. Anything, I don't care just so it pays the rent and buys me food. I've already tried to get on welfare. The answer was, why don't I catch a man and let him support me?"

"There are a lot of people in your fix."

"Don't I know it!"

"Maybe if we all stood up on our hind legs and hollered, things would be spread around fairer. You know there's plenty of everything; some people are grabbing it all." He smiled apologetically. "That doesn't put food on your table, does it? We have to feed people right now. While we try to change the system."

That sounded like some of Thea's talk. Must be a lot of it around, a lot of people thinking about these things. If enough people thought about them, would they find an answer?

She wished he knew Thea. He sounded like Thea after she had been talking to her friends at the bookstore. She wondered where those ideas came from, how they got spread around, and if many people were thinking along these lines.

"Welfare only got started in the depression, you know." He was reading her mind. "Social Security and Medicare came along later. Maybe we'll get civilized some day — if some fool doesn't push the button first."

He had brought back, besides the cold drinks, a green box full of index cards. Now he began going through them, rapidly. He pulled one. "If you'll excuse me, I'll make a phone call. Now the kids are all out." He shook his head. "It's an awful age, no longer tadpole and not yet frog."

How long was it since she had played basketball? Not since grade school. She wondered if they had teams for grownups.

He came back, looking pleased. "It's no position, but if you'll work for legal minimum you can start Monday morning. Little restaurant on Speedway — you can get there by bus? Good. Some waitressing, some cleanup, some kitchen work. How are you on salads? Good. A lot of vegetarians eat there. Thirty hours a week, and you get lunch." He wrote on another index card and handed it to her.

She took it and thanked him, feeling unreal.

"Don't be surprised if some of the kitchen help scuttles out the back way all of a sudden and you're left to fill in. There are some people in town who don't like certain accents."

She was halfway home before she began to wonder what he was talking about.

She put on her best slacks and shirt to interview the manager of the Flower Garden, but she needn't have bothered. People seemed to wear whatever they wanted to — jeans, shorts, long full cotton skirts. The girls were mostly younger than she was, and everybody seemed to wear sandals. There would be no uniforms to buy. A very young and obviously gay man — boy, really — played flute from time to time, apparently whenever he felt like it, in a corner of the dining room. The customers were mostly young, and those who ate alone mostly had books propped up in front of them. She guessed some of them were gay, but it was hard to tell with this casual southwestern style of dressing. Thea said gay people were always starting styles and straights were always imitating them.

She was going to like this, and she could easily do the work — nobody seemed to be in any hurry. As for the money, it was too good to believe. She would figure it out later, when she wasn't so busy.

There was a thin blonde waitress called Deena that she liked right from the start. Something about her reminded Marty of Thea, though they didn't look alike, really. On the second day she asked, "Do you ever go to the women's bookstore?" and Deena laughed. "That's where all my money goes. They've got the best selection of feminist books in the state."

Marty glowed, as if she had been complimented.

She had been there a week when a thin shabby boy came barreling in the back way and spoke to the chef. He nodded, spoon in hand. The boy went quickly through the kitchen, speaking to one and another — four in all. Silently, they walked out through the restaurant, between the tables, and out the front door. Nobody seemed to pay any attention. A minute later, when two stocky men in uniform pounded on the back door, everyone was busy — busier than Marty had ever seen them before. The chef was washing lettuce, which was certainly not his job. The flute boy was filling ketchup bottles, the only real work Marty had ever seen him do.

"Border patrol," one of the men said in a businesslike voice. "We're looking for Arturo Mendez, Rafael Gonzales," and some other names Marty didn't catch.

Jack said, "I don't know. I'll call the manager," and George came in, transformed into Mr. Holly by putting on a jacket and a dignified manner. The two men took him into a corner and talked to him. A few minutes later they went away, looking angry but not surprised.

"He should have kept them a little longer," the chef said.

Deena nodded. "It's all right though, they're home by now."

Marty said, "Will somebody tell me what that was about?"

They looked at her. One of the thin young waitresses put down a plate of pastries. "Joe Jardine sent you here, didn't he? I guess you're okay. The border guards are looking for some of our folks, that's all."

"Wetbacks?" She knew about wetbacks from Rico.

"Not exactly. We call them undocumented refugees. Some people say illegal aliens."

"The INS is really breaking the law," Deena explained. "The government of this country signed the Helsinki Accords, the Geneva Convention, saying people in danger of their lives at home should be given refugee status. Let into the country, given jobs, residential permits, all that stuff. Only Reagan and his buddies are on the other side. They arrest them and send them back to where they came from."

The flute boy said, "*They're* breaking the law, not us."

Later, as they walked towards the bus stop, Deena filled in a little. "You know the skinny kid they call Joe? He's really Arturo — you heard the INS man ask about him. He came home from a union meeting one night and found his whole family shot and his house burned down. It was against the law in El Salvador to belong to a union. What happens if they catch him and send him back? Death or jail."

They got on the bus and dropped their fares in the box. "There's places all along the way, safe houses, and people from the different churches get them across the border and find places for them to stay."

The undocumented refugees were back on the job the next day. Nobody mentioned what had happened.

Chapter 21

"Are you working tomorrow?"

Marty shook her head. "Are you?"

"No, it's mostly students on weekends. George thinks it's better for a lot of people to work some than for a few to work a lot."

That was an economic theory Marty could understand and agree with. Deena counted out bus fare. "Are you going to the rally, then?"

"I didn't know there was one."

"Himmel Park, from ten o'clock, all day probably. Coalition for Justice in Central America. There'll probably be a lot of speakers on other things, everybody gets into the act at rallies, but that's the big one. Gay rights and disarmament and save the whales — you know. There'll be refreshments to buy and music and maybe a short march, or something. I always come away with a few more buttons." Deena looked at her. "My roommate says I could open a button store."

"How would I get there?"

"Brenda and Jackie are going to pick us up. They can probably squeeze you in — always room for one more."

"I don't see why not." Sunday was a bad day; after she ate breakfast and went to see the Ruiz family there was nothing to do; she had been eating breakfast at McDonald's because the house felt so empty. "Where do you hear about these things? 'Course, I don't see a paper."

Deena looked at her in disbelief. "There's over thirty peace organizations in this town. You sign up to be put on a mailing list."

That didn't make sense to Marty until she scrambled out of the small overcrowded car and saw the long line of tables stretching down both sides of a walkway. Everyone had a sign: Women's International League for Peace and Freedom, American Friends Service Committee, Catholic Workers House, Tucson AIDS Project — she wondered if Juan knew there was such a thing. Twenty or more groups, and every table was spread with tee shirts, buttons, bumper stickers, books for sale and papers for free, petitions to sign, mailing lists — she signed the first one she came to. There were glass jugs clinking with lemonade and ice, plates of chocolate brownies, muffins, barbecue made of tofu — she had never tasted tofu, but they served it at the Flower Garden and she reminded herself to try it for free. She had never seen anything like it.

A boy handed her a paper called *The Daily World.* Someone else gave her a sheet announcing a folk concert. Several people spoke to her, though she couldn't remember ever having see any of them before. A young man said, "We're going to walk around the block and stand by the curb. Grab a sign."

Her sign said, "Nicaragua is not our enemy" in big black letters. That was all right, as far as she knew nobody was her enemy. She stood by the edge of the street with about thirty other people and held her sign, and cars going past honked, and the picketers waved back. It was a good feeling.

The other picnickers were mostly young, although there was a scattering of old people looking relaxed and cheerful. Some of the young ones carried babies. Little kids ran around playing tag games. Even the dogs that made their way through the groups of people looked good-natured. Where had everyone come from? They looked different from the people she saw everyday, friendly and casual and alert. Maybe having a day off and being outdoors was what made them look that way.

A girl said, "Ted's going to sing." A short young man in bib overalls, with a long black beard and long black hair, climbed up on the improvised platform carrying a guitar, and the buzz of talk softened, though it didn't stop. From the scatter of applause while he was tuning up, it was apparent that they knew him and liked him. Marty found a folding chair and sat down.

People were sprawled on the grass, standing around in little bunches. Some had brought folding lawn chairs. Ted sang. The music was sort of like hymns and sort of political speeches set to music — she had never heard anything like it. It certainly wasn't like the music you heard on TV and radio. Anyway, she could understand every word, so it couldn't have been what they called classical music. Some of the listeners sang along. Some clapped their hands in time to the music. A little girl sitting down front clapped solemnly; she looked about three or four years old. One of the songs was about being poor and out of work. "Give me back my old job, mister," the man in overalls sang. "I don't want your millions, mister, I don't want your diamond ring." Exactly what she had thought a hundred times, and here was somebody else who had thought it too and made a song out of it.

A brown-skinned man got up on the platform and talked about Palestinian rights. There was polite applause. Another young man, with a heavy accent like the guys in the restaurant kitchen, told about getting out of Guatemala. He looked Mexican, or perhaps more Indian; he was younger than Rico, and he had seen people killed and tortured and raped, a priest killed at the altar and his body dragged out into the street. It was like something in a horror movie, barbarians riding into a village and sacking it. She looked around at the people listening intently, the clear blue sky with floating white clouds and the long tables, and it was hard to believe, but she couldn't doubt that it was true.

Three young people with instruments she had never seen before played some sad low-pitched music. A little girl shook two gourds in time with the grownups.

An old lady on crutches hobbled up to the front of the group and stood near the platform while someone lowered the mike so she wouldn't have to climb up. She talked about the terrible condition of health care in Arizona, how the county hospital no longer offered free care and the poor couldn't get a doctor when they needed one. This was something Marty knew about.

"I speak as a Social Security recipient," the old lady said in a loud clear voice. "Last year we got a raise of one and one third percent to offset inflation, but the actual inflation was between ten and twelve percent and our dollar has lost a tenth of its purchasing power. We need free clinics, dental care, glasses. The young people in the community, the unemployed and little children need health care and an adequate diet." Marty joined in the applause, remembering the little graves in the Mexican cemetery and the dolls and teddy bears in the memorial boxes.

The young man in bib overalls sang again. This time the songs were about war, what the government was doing to push the country into war, and they were funny but they were grimly true, too. There was an intermission during which people walked around and bought things to eat. Marty had a fudge brownie and then, because it made her thirsty, a glass of sun tea. It was pretty good, though not very cold. She looked around for Deena, didn't see her anywhere, but didn't worry — someone would find her when it was time to leave. She picked up a handful of leaflets and spent half a dollar on a button that said I LIKE UPPITY WOMEN. That made her think of Thea, and for a lonesome homesick moment she wished Thea were there with her.

A small fair-haired woman came up to her. "Is your name Marty Brown, by chance?"

"Well, yes, it is."

"Mountaintop said she thought it was you. My name's Gillian. I run the feminist bookstore."

She had pictured a feminist bookstore owner as — she didn't know what — big and dykey, a stomping butch, or skinny and dried-out. This girl in white shorts and a tee shirt printed *Listen to Women for a Change* looked like somebody's kid sister. Marty didn't know what to say to her. The silence lingered.

This woman knew about the things Thea had tried to tell her. She would know where Palestine was, why death squads were gunning down farmers and priests, how people could organize free clinics. All of the people in the park knew about these things, and they cared. They were here on their day off to exchange their knowledge and figure out some answers. Probably they didn't all know each other — she had never met any of them before, but they treated her like a friend.

A small naked child of about two tripped and fell. Marty stooped to pick her up, and the kid's mother gave her a beautiful smile.

"I'm a friend of Thea's," Gillian said, having looked Marty up and down and all over. "She's here someplace. I think she'd like to see you."

That took the wind out of Marty. She couldn't have answered if she had known what to say.

"You wait right here. I'll see if I can find her."

Marty's knees were shaking. She wanted to run, and couldn't move. It was like those dreams where something is chasing you and your feet are stuck to the ground.

Thea and Gillian came back hand-in-hand, like sisters. Thea's face looked as scared as Marty felt, but she walked steadily and her eyes were fixed on Marty's. Gillian gave them a small smile and walked away.

Thea said, "I wanted to talk to you."

Marty nodded.

"Come over in the shade."

They crossed a stretch of coarse desert grass, dodging between groups of people. The sun was high now; it was October, but it felt more like July. Fat white clouds floated across an improbably blue sky. Thea found a stretch of grass and sat down, not minding the dust that rose from under her. Marty dropped down beside her. For a long moment, neither of them said anything.

"I owe you an apology," Thea said at last, in such a low voice Marty could hardly hear her. "I shouldn't have run off like that. I should have given you a chance to explain."

"Nothing to explain. I made a damn fool of myself. I was sneaky and dishonest and dumb."

"Yes, you were. I should have given you a chance, just the same. I'm too quick on the trigger."

"I was cheating."

"Your life belongs to you."

That was worse than anger — she didn't care.

"Rico asked me if we were monogamous."

"What did you tell him?"

"Told him I didn't know, we never talked about it."

"Maybe the time for talk has come."

Marty said, without meaning to, "I never really wanted anybody but you. Joan was like a dream, like something I was watching on TV, and you were like real life. Good but not so romantic. It was like those old stories where somebody drinks some wine, or something, and gets changed into — into —"

"Pigs," Thea said straight-faced. "That was Ulysses."

"Well, whoever."

Thea smiled. "It's all right. You never loved me, I was just something that happened, and then this beautiful woman came along."

Marty's head jerked back. "How do you mean I never loved you? I was too worried and all to think about it. I didn't know till after you walked out on me. Love isn't a roll in a motel bed, it's everything you have together."

"Oh, me too, Marty, I've learned a lot since I've been with Rollingearth and Mountaintop. They don't believe in monogamy. I could have gone to bed with either of them, it wouldn't have hurt their relationship, because they have so much else. But I didn't want to." She swallowed hard. "Maybe I will sometime. Maybe I'll find someone who really cares about me, and is interested in the same things I am.

I'm on the gay telephone hotline, I'm doing volunteer work for the AIDS program. Till I find a longtime lover, will you forgive me and be friends?"

"Nothing to forgive. How can I forgive you when I was the one to blame? I'd better ask will you forgive me?"

Thea said in a burst of anger, "This can go on forever, you forgive me, I forgive you. Why don't we just start over and find out?"

Marty almost stopped breathing. "How do you mean? Would you come back to the barrio and see if we could do better, make a real relationship?"

"Oh, we could both do better. And yes, I'd probably come back if you really want me to. I miss the neighborhood, and Mama Ruiz and the boys. I even miss the food boxes."

"I'm working now, at the Flower Garden. Did you know they have a lot of refugees working there? They're really good people."

"I still don't have a job. I'm auditing some courses — no credit — and I've put in for a grant. I still get the welfare checks; I've been giving Mountaintop something every week for my food." Thea grinned. "I go out and buy a hamburger every once in awhile, I'm not a very good vegetarian." Her face grew solemn. "One of the grants I've applied for is for five thousand dollars — to do a survey for a string of storefront clinics. I'd sell my soul to do that survey. Think of it, doctors and nurses giving their time to take care of poor and homeless people."

"Maybe they'd have something I could do, weekends."

"Sure they would."

They looked at each other in a sizing-up way. Thea said, "It would be fun to work together."

"It would be fun to go to bed and make love together."

"Yes, it would. Only no promises, no commitments. Just doing what we can, one day at a time. I'd like to try."

"You're better than I am, and smarter too. You're the best thing that ever happened to me."

"You're you and I'm me," Thea said sternly. "Only if you get magicked by someone else I hope you'll say so. Same with me. There's nothing we can't talk over."

They looked at each other. Thea began to smile. "Even if we don't stay lovers forever, we'll always be sisters."

"Maybe we can be both."

They stood up and leaned together. Marty thought, for a moment, that they were going to kiss. Then they moved apart, and the look they gave each other was better than a kiss. Their hands reached out and gripped. Marty said, "Let's give it a try."

"Why not? There isn't so much love in the world. We can't afford to waste any."

They walked back to the speaker's platform, where another music group was tuning up.

Mountaintop saw them go past, not noticing her because they were looking at each other. Maybe they'll make it, she thought. Goddess knows it's not easy being gay in a straight world, and being broke makes it harder, but maybe they'll make it this time. I sure hope they will.

She went off to tell Rollingearth.

A few of the publications of
THE NAIAD PRESS, INC.
P.O. Box 10543 ● Tallahassee, Florida 32302
Phone (904) 539-5965
Mail orders welcome. Please include 15% postage.

CHRIS by Randy Salem. 224 pp. Golden oldie. Handsome Chris
and her adventures.   ISBN 0-941483-42-8 $8.95

THREE WOMEN by Sally Singer. 232 pp. Golden oldie. A
triangle among wealthy sophisticates. ISBN 0-941483-43-6   8.95

RICE AND BEANS by Valeria Taylor. 232 pp. Love and
romance on poverty row.   ISBN 0-941483-41-X   8.95

PLEASURES by Robbi Sommers. 204 pp. Unprecedented
eroticism.   ISBN 0-941483-49-5   8.95

EDGEWISE by Camarin Grae. 372 pp. Spellbinding
adventure.   ISBN 0-941483-19-3   9.95

FATAL REUNION by Claire McNab. 216 pp. 2nd Det. Inspec.
Carol Ashton mystery.   ISBN 0-941483-40-1   8.95

KEEP TO ME STRANGER by Sarah Aldridge. 372 pp. Romance
set in a department store dynasty.   ISBN 0-941483-38-X   9.95

HEARTSCAPE by Sue Gambill. 204 pp. American lesbian in
Portugal.   ISBN 0-941483-33-9   8.95

IN THE BLOOD by Lauren Wright Douglas. 252 pp. Lesbian
science fiction adventure fantasy   ISBN 0-941483-22-3   8.95

THE BEE'S KISS by Shirley Verel. 216 pp. Delicate, delicious
romance.   ISBN 0-941483-36-3   8.95

RAGING MOTHER MOUNTAIN by Pat Emmerson. 264 pp.
Furosa Firechild's adventures in Wonderland. ISBN 0-941483-35-5 8.95

IN EVERY PORT by Karin Kallmaker. 228 pp. Jessica's sexy,
adventuresome travels.   ISBN 0-941483-37-7   8.95

OF LOVE AND GLORY by Evelyn Kennedy. 192 pp. Exciting
WWII romance.   ISBN 0-941483-32-0   8.95

CLICKING STONES by Nancy Tyler Glenn. 288 pp. Love
transcending time.   ISBN 0-941483-31-2   8.95

SURVIVING SISTERS by Gail Pass. 252 pp. Powerful love
story.   ISBN 0-941483-16-9   8.95

SOUTH OF THE LINE by Catherine Ennis. 216 pp. Civil War
adventure.   ISBN 0-941483-29-0   8.95

WOMAN PLUS WOMAN by Dolores Klaich. 300 pp. Supurb
Lesbian overview.   ISBN 0-941483-28-2   9.95

SLOW DANCING AT MISS POLLY'S by Sheila Ortiz Taylor.
96 pp. Lesbian Poetry   ISBN 0-941483-30-4   7.95

DOUBLE DAUGHTER by Vicki P. McConnell. 216 pp. A Nyla
Wade Mystery, third in the series.   ISBN 0-941483-26-6   8.95

HEAVY GILT by Delores Klaich. 192 pp. Lesbian detective/
disappearing homophobes/upper class gay society.
                                           ISBN 0-941483-25-8   8.95

THE FINER GRAIN by Denise Ohio. 216 pp. Brilliant young
college lesbian novel.   ISBN 0-941483-11-8   8.95

THE AMAZON TRAIL by Lee Lynch. 216 pp. Life, travel & lore
of famous lesbian author.   ISBN 0-941483-27-4   8.95

HIGH CONTRAST by Jessie Lattimore. 264 pp. Women of the
Crystal Palace.   ISBN 0-941483-17-7   8.95

OCTOBER OBSESSION by Meredith More. Josie's rich, secret
Lesbian life.   ISBN 0-941483-18-5   8.95

LESBIAN CROSSROADS by Ruth Baetz. 276 pp. Contemporary
Lesbian lives.   ISBN 0-941483-21-5   9.95

BEFORE STONEWALL: THE MAKING OF A GAY AND
LESBIAN COMMUNITY by Andrea Weiss & Greta Schiller.
96 pp., 25 illus.   ISBN 0-941483-20-7   7.95

WE WALK THE BACK OF THE TIGER by Patricia A. Murphy.
192 pp. Romantic Lesbian novel/beginning women's movement.
                                           ISBN 0-941483-13-4   8.95

SUNDAY'S CHILD by Joyce Bright. 216 pp. Lesbian athletics, at
last the novel about sports.   ISBN 0-941483-12-6   8.95

OSTEN'S BAY by Zenobia N. Vole. 204 pp. Sizzling adventure
romance set on Bonaire.   ISBN 0-941483-15-0   8.95

LESSONS IN MURDER by Claire McNab. 216 pp. 1st Det. Inspec.
Carol Ashton mystery — erotic tension!.   ISBN 0-941483-14-2   8.95

YELLOWTHROAT by Penny Hayes. 240 pp. Margarita, bandit,
kidnaps Julia.   ISBN 0-941483-10-X   8.95

SAPPHISTRY: THE BOOK OF LESBIAN SEXUALITY by
Pat Califia. 3d edition, revised. 208 pp. ISBN 0-941483-24-X   8.95

CHERISHED LOVE by Evelyn Kennedy. 192 pp. Erotic
Lesbian love story.   ISBN 0-941483-08-8   8.95

LAST SEPTEMBER by Helen R. Hull. 208 pp. Six stories & a
glorious novella.   ISBN 0-941483-09-6   8.95

THE SECRET IN THE BIRD by Camarin Grae. 312 pp. Striking,
psychological suspense novel.   ISBN 0-941483-05-3   8.95

TO THE LIGHTNING by Catherine Ennis. 208 pp. Romantic
Lesbian 'Robinson Crusoe' adventure.   ISBN 0-941483-06-1   8.95

THE OTHER SIDE OF VENUS by Shirley Verel. 224 pp.
Luminous, romantic love story.   ISBN 0-941483-07-X   8.95

DREAMS AND SWORDS by Katherine V. Forrest. 192 pp.
Romantic, erotic, imaginative stories.   ISBN 0-941483-03-7   8.95

MEMORY BOARD by Jane Rule. 336 pp. Memorable novel
about an aging Lesbian couple.   ISBN 0-941483-02-9   8.95

THE ALWAYS ANONYMOUS BEAST by Lauren Wright
Douglas. 224 pp. A Caitlin Reese mystery. First in a series.
                                        ISBN 0-941483-04-5   8.95

SEARCHING FOR SPRING by Patricia A. Murphy. 224 pp.
Novel about the recovery of love.   ISBN 0-941483-00-2   8.95

DUSTY'S QUEEN OF HEARTS DINER by Lee Lynch. 240 pp.
Romantic blue-collar novel.   ISBN 0-941483-01-0   8.95

PARENTS MATTER by Ann Muller. 240 pp. Parents'
relationships with Lesbian daughters and gay sons.
                                        ISBN 0-930044-91-6   9.95

THE PEARLS by Shelley Smith. 176 pp. Passion and fun in
the Caribbean sun.   ISBN 0-930044-93-2   7.95

MAGDALENA by Sarah Aldridge. 352 pp. Epic Lesbian novel
set on three continents.   ISBN 0-930044-99-1   8.95

THE BLACK AND WHITE OF IT by Ann Allen Shockley.
144 pp. Short stories.   ISBN 0-930044-96-7   7.95

SAY JESUS AND COME TO ME by Ann Allen Shockley. 288
pp. Contemporary romance.   ISBN 0-930044-98-3   8.95

LOVING HER by Ann Allen Shockley. 192 pp. Romantic love
story.   ISBN 0-930044-97-5   7.95

MURDER AT THE NIGHTWOOD BAR by Katherine V.
Forrest. 240 pp. A Kate Delafield mystery. Second in a series.
                                        ISBN 0-930044-92-4   8.95

ZOE'S BOOK by Gail Pass. 224 pp. Passionate, obsessive love
story.   ISBN 0-930044-95-9   7.95

WINGED DANCER by Camarin Grae. 228 pp. Erotic Lesbian
adventure story.   ISBN 0-930044-88-6   8.95

PAZ by Camarin Grae. 336 pp. Romantic Lesbian adventurer
with the power to change the world.   ISBN 0-930044-89-4   8.95

SOUL SNATCHER by Camarin Grae. 224 pp. A puzzle, an
adventure, a mystery — Lesbian romance.   ISBN 0-930044-90-8   8.95

THE LOVE OF GOOD WOMEN by Isabel Miller. 224 pp.
Long-awaited new novel by the author of the beloved *Patience
and Sarah*.   ISBN 0-930044-81-9   8.95

THE HOUSE AT PELHAM FALLS by Brenda Weathers. 240
pp. Suspenseful Lesbian ghost story.   ISBN 0-930044-79-7   7.95

HOME IN YOUR HANDS by Lee Lynch. 240 pp. More stories
from the author of *Old Dyke Tales*.   ISBN 0-930044-80-0   7.95

EACH HAND A MAP by Anita Skeen. 112 pp. Real-life poems that touch us all. ISBN 0-930044-82-7   6.95

SURPLUS by Sylvia Stevenson. 342 pp. A classic early Lesbian novel. ISBN 0-930044-78-9   7.95

PEMBROKE PARK by Michelle Martin. 256 pp. Derring-do and daring romance in Regency England. ISBN 0-930044-77-0   7.95

THE LONG TRAIL by Penny Hayes. 248 pp. Vivid adventures of two women in love in the old west. ISBN 0-930044-76-2   8.95

HORIZON OF THE HEART by Shelley Smith. 192 pp. Hot romance in summertime New England. ISBN 0-930044-75-4   7.95

AN EMERGENCE OF GREEN by Katherine V. Forrest. 288 pp. Powerful novel of sexual discovery. ISBN 0-930044-69-X   8.95

THE LESBIAN PERIODICALS INDEX edited by Claire Potter. 432 pp. Author & subject index. ISBN 0-930044-74-6   29.95

DESERT OF THE HEART by Jane Rule. 224 pp. A classic; basis for the movie *Desert Hearts*. ISBN 0-930044-73-8   7.95

SPRING FORWARD/FALL BACK by Sheila Ortiz Taylor. 288 pp. Literary novel of timeless love. ISBN 0-930044-70-3   7.95

FOR KEEPS by Elisabeth Nonas. 144 pp. Contemporary novel about losing and finding love. ISBN 0-930044-71-1   7.95

TORCHLIGHT TO VALHALLA by Gale Wilhelm. 128 pp. Classic novel by a great Lesbian writer. ISBN 0-930044-68-1   7.95

LESBIAN NUNS: BREAKING SILENCE edited by Rosemary Curb and Nancy Manahan. 432 pp. Unprecedented autobiographies of religious life. ISBN 0-930044-62-2   9.95

THE SWASHBUCKLER by Lee Lynch. 288 pp. Colorful novel set in Greenwich Village in the sixties. ISBN 0-930044-66-5   8.95

MISFORTUNE'S FRIEND by Sarah Aldridge. 320 pp. Historical Lesbian novel set on two continents. ISBN 0-930044-67-3   7.95

A STUDIO OF ONE'S OWN by Ann Stokes. Edited by Dolores Klaich. 128 pp. Autobiography. ISBN 0-930044-64-9   7.95

SEX VARIANT WOMEN IN LITERATURE by Jeannette Howard Foster. 448 pp. Literary history. ISBN 0-930044-65-7   8.95

A HOT-EYED MODERATE by Jane Rule. 252 pp. Hard-hitting essays on gay life; writing; art. ISBN 0-930044-57-6   7.95

INLAND PASSAGE AND OTHER STORIES by Jane Rule. 288 pp. Wide-ranging new collection. ISBN 0-930044-56-8   7.95

WE TOO ARE DRIFTING by Gale Wilhelm. 128 pp. Timeless Lesbian novel, a masterpiece. ISBN 0-930044-61-4   6.95

AMATEUR CITY by Katherine V. Forrest. 224 pp. A Kate Delafield mystery. First in a series. ISBN 0-930044-55-X   7.95

THE SOPHIE HOROWITZ STORY by Sarah Schulman. 176 pp. Engaging novel of madcap intrigue.   ISBN 0-930044-54-1   7.95

THE BURNTON WIDOWS by Vickie P. McConnell. 272 pp. A Nyla Wade mystery, second in the series.   ISBN 0-930044-52-5   7.95

OLD DYKE TALES by Lee Lynch. 224 pp. Extraordinary stories of our diverse Lesbian lives.   ISBN 0-930044-51-7   8.95

DAUGHTERS OF A CORAL DAWN by Katherine V. Forrest. 240 pp. Novel set in a Lesbian new world.   ISBN 0-930044-50-9   7.95

THE PRICE OF SALT by Claire Morgan. 288 pp. A milestone novel, a beloved classic.   ISBN 0-930044-49-5   8.95

AGAINST THE SEASON by Jane Rule. 224 pp. Luminous, complex novel of interrelationships.   ISBN 0-930044-48-7   8.95

LOVERS IN THE PRESENT AFTERNOON by Kathleen Fleming. 288 pp. A novel about recovery and growth.   ISBN 0-930044-46-0   8.95

TOOTHPICK HOUSE by Lee Lynch. 264 pp. Love between two Lesbians of different classes.   ISBN 0-930044-45-2   7.95

MADAME AURORA by Sarah Aldridge. 256 pp. Historical novel featuring a charismatic "seer."   ISBN 0-930044-44-4   7.95

CURIOUS WINE by Katherine V. Forrest. 176 pp. Passionate Lesbian love story, a best-seller.   ISBN 0-930044-43-6   8.95

BLACK LESBIAN IN WHITE AMERICA by Anita Cornwell. 141 pp. Stories, essays, autobiography.   ISBN 0-930044-41-X   7.50

CONTRACT WITH THE WORLD by Jane Rule. 340 pp. Powerful, panoramic novel of gay life.   ISBN 0-930044-28-2   7.95

MRS. PORTER'S LETTER by Vicki P. McConnell. 224 pp. The first Nyla Wade mystery.   ISBN 0-930044-29-0   7.95

TO THE CLEVELAND STATION by Carol Anne Douglas. 192 pp. Interracial Lesbian love story.   ISBN 0-930044-27-4   6.95

THE NESTING PLACE by Sarah Aldridge. 224 pp. A three-woman triangle—love conquers all!   ISBN 0-930044-26-6   7.95

THIS IS NOT FOR YOU by Jane Rule. 284 pp. A letter to a beloved is also an intricate novel.   ISBN 0-930044-25-8   8.95

FAULTLINE by Sheila Ortiz Taylor. 140 pp. Warm, funny, literate story of a startling family.   ISBN 0-930044-24-X   6.95

These are just a few of the many Naiad Press titles — we are the oldest and largest lesbian/feminist publishing company in the world. Please request a complete catalog. We offer personal service; we encourage and welcome direct mail orders from individuals who have limited access to bookstores carrying our publications.